Other Books by
ALFRED McCLUNG LEE

The Daily Newspaper in America: The Evolution of a
   Social Instrument

The Fine Art of Propaganda (with Elizabeth Briant Lee)

Social Problems in America (with Elizabeth Briant Lee)

Principles of Sociology (editor, co-author)

Readings in Sociology (editor, co-author)

How to Understand Propaganda

Public Opinion and Propaganda (co-editor, co-author)

Fraternities Without Brotherhood

La Sociologia delle Comunicazioni (UNESCO lectures)

Che Cos'è la Propaganda (Fulbright lectures)

Marriage and the Family (with Elizabeth Briant Lee)

Multivalent Man

RACE RIOT

(DETROIT, 1943)

by

ALFRED McCLUNG LEE

and

NORMAN D. HUMPHREY

With a new introductory essay by
ALFRED McCLUNG LEE

1968

OCTAGON BOOKS, INC.
New York

Reprinted 1968
by special arrangement with Alfred McClung Lee
and Mrs. Elizabeth R. Weible

OCTAGON BOOKS, INC.
175 FIFTH AVENUE
NEW YORK, N. Y. 10010

LIBRARY OF CONGRESS CATALOG CARD NUMBER: 68-20841

Printed in U.S.A. by
NOBLE OFFSET PRINTERS, INC.
NEW YORK 3, N. Y.

TO

BETTY

Introduction to the Octagon Edition

RACE RIOTS ARE SYMPTOMS

by ALFRED McCLUNG LEE

Riot reports in press and on television slash holes—for the time—in the Bandana Curtain. Murders, lootings, and burnings force whites to see and even to feel—for the time—that "something is wrong" in our Negro ghettos. But in spite of the repeated and disastrous riots in major American cities during the "long hot summers" of the mid-1960's, perceptive analysts doubt that our political and business leaders have as yet actually "got the message."

Prejudiced and easy answers aside, why have police and Negroes been rioting in our cities? How can we all come to an adequate understanding of the settings for those appalling jamborees of violence?

The bandana symbolizes for Negroes the persistence of the idea of the "good nigger," of the female "bandana head" (the bandana-turbaned Aunt Jemima), the mate of the obsequious Uncle Tom. Whites have traditionally assumed that Aunt Jemima and Uncle Tom are not stereotypes but real people who happily and fully know and accept "their places" in the white man's world. All too often, whites insist that deviations from those roles are pathological and thus threats to the white scheme of things, called the "established order." Negroes, for their part, have long lived with the rankling degradation of pressures to force them to perform such roles. Even when they appear to act such parts, they are play-acting; they cannot permit such strait-jackets to become part of themselves. As the poet Paul Laurence Dunbar[1] chants,

> We smile, but O great Christ, our cries
> To thee from tortured souls arise. . . .
> But let the world dream otherwise;
> We wear the mask.

The Negro journalist Lerone Bennett, Jr.,[2] puts it more bitterly:

> For more than four hundred years, the Negro has looked out on
> America from the prison of a mask. He has manipulated the
> mask, dropping it suddenly, becoming refractory and threaten-
> ing, putting it on again, becoming conciliatory and charming,
> pushing it to one side, trying on new hats and new roles, admir-
> ing himself in the mirror of tempting but forbidden self-con-
> ceptions. For more than four hundred years, the Negro has
> wavered between the hot poles of submission and revolt.

Through the Bandana Curtain, which is less opaque for them,
Negroes see little that endears the white community to them. Even
gestures of liberals and humanitarians in aid of the Negroes so lack
persistence, consistency, and decisiveness that they tend chiefly to
provide still other stimulations to frustration. Through the Bandana
Curtain, even when torn by riot reports, whites see little, and what
they see is distorted. The Bandana Curtain is a barrier of myth, fan-
tasy, wishful thinking, and social distance that sharply separates the
white and Negro communities. It makes accurate communication from
one to the other exceedingly difficult.

Some rioters deliberately murder, loot, and burn for private gain or
group advantage. Some have mental problems. Some are hardened
criminals. A great many more—the vast majority of rioters—get swept
into mob destructiveness to give vent to their life-long frustrations.
More specifically, they are impelled to get even with representatives
of those who have cheated, exploited, and belittled them in the past.
These representatives are the police and the merchants. But all of us
participate directly or indirectly in any riot in our society and especially in a slum riot. All of us share responsibility for the conditions of
which riots are but symptoms.

Negroes did not accept or remain in slavery willingly. "From the
moment of their enslavement the Negroes did not stop resisting; in
the slave barracoons of the West Coast [of Africa], on shipboard and
on the plantations there was a persistent danger of revolt that made
life a nightmare to those in charge of these Negroes."[3] More than 200
slave conspiracies and revolts are reported during the two centuries
prior to the Civil War.[4] Even though only a few of these revolts assumed the proportions of an insurrection and none could be called
successful, the attempts "were frequent enough to keep the South in

constant fear and to create a real problem of slave control." And then
came the Civil War and with it the "greatest and most successful slave
revolt—a sort of general strike against slavery. . . . The Union armies
thus obtained many valuable informers and well over 100,000 recruits."[5]

During the century since the Civil War, sporadic violence between
whites and Negroes continues to symptomize the deep-set tensions
between the two communities. "Reconstruction was in a sense a prolonged race riot" in which at least 5,000 Negroes died.[6] Some 5,000
more Negroes were lynched since Reconstruction.[7] After the Civil War,
interracial riots took the place of slave uprisings, particularly after
1880, as mediums of interracial conflict. They began more with the
character of white raids and then became more and more Negro revolts. Twelve died in the 1906 Atlanta riot, and six in the 1908 Springfield (Illinois) riot. From 1913 to 1963, 76 race riots shook American
cities, towns, and army installations.[8] The 1917 riot in East St. Louis
(Illinois) took about 48 lives.[9] Of the 26 riots in 1919, the one in
Chicago cost 38 lives,[10] and the one in Phillips County (Arkansas),
some 25 to 50. And then came such others as the Detroit riots of 1925,
1942, and 1943, the Harlem riots of 1935 and 1943, and, after a gap of
comparative quiet, the bloody summers of 1964-67. American Negroes
have never lived contentedly under oppression, and American whites
have yet to permit them to work openly, effectively, and without interference toward equal status.

Will the rioting continue? Will there be more long, hot summers of
violence in our cities? On the eve of the 1943 riots, even such a careful
group of students as Gunner Myrdal and his associates[11] concluded
that the "future looks fairly peaceful in the North" and that the "deva-
station and relative fewness [of riots] make them landmarks in history."
Even in 1963, another thoughtful student[12] of riots could note accurately that "the last major race riot took place over two decades ago....
The Negro protest for equal status, although generating controversy,
recrimination, and even conflict, has thus far occurred without a major
race riot." Now, with the hindsight given us by the horrors of the past
four summers, we may lean in the other direction in speculating about
the future. As an informed Washington official[13] asserted after the
1967 Detroit riot, "There will be more Detroits." In considering how
far short Negroes still remain of effective and functioning equality of
opportunity, the psychologist Kenneth B. Clark[14] states: "The riots

themselves are the best evaluations of what's been done." Such evalua-
ations in the future will depend on what Negroes can actually accomplish in American society by nonviolent means.

Thus, the social history of the Negro in this country does not include
a stable, idyllic past of many fine masters and herds of devoted slaves,
destroyed by the cupidity and brutality of a few unprincipled planta-
tion overlords and deviantly incorrigible bondmen. The contention of
the Southern journalist Hodding Carter[15] that "the new Negro has
robbed all of us of something, a good many somethings, that were
beautiful and inspiring and unique," can scarcely arouse in a Negro
old or new a friendly response. Carter and his like see a very special
version of Negro personalities and social life as they think they once
were and as they think they still should be. This Bandana Curtain
version is pleasing to nostalgic whites but forever bitter to Negroes.

Even when masters were kind, Negroes resented them as much as
our white ancestors resented the special powers of their manorial lords
in Europe. Few human beings can accept without resentment a sub-
ordination from which they cannot escape by legitimate means—
whether that of slavery or that of the urban ghetto. A Northern white
asked an escaped slave, "Why, then, did you run away? If your master
was kind, you had plenty to eat, and were not overworked, why did
you leave?" To this the Negro replied, "Well, boss, de place am open
if you wants to take it."[16] Or, as a young Negro militant[17] uttered a
similar point recently in Detroit:

> Yeah, sure, Jerry Baby's [Detroit Mayor Jerome P. Cavanagh's]
> done a few things for us. . . . But that's just it, man. We're tired
> of having people do things for us. We want to do things for
> ourselves. I mean this isn't way down yonder in New Orleans
> any more, and we don't need any nice old plantation sugar
> daddy to take care of us. We're going to help ourselves whether
> whitey likes it or not. And that's just what Jerry Baby and all
> those other nice white liberals don't like. They're willing to
> share some of the corn and taters with us, but when it gets
> right down to the nitty-gritty of power, they aren't sharing
> anything.

An old Danish proverb—echoed in most other lands—makes the same
point in a few words: "Better to be a free bird than a captive king."

To what can we more specifically attribute the crescendo of Negro

demand for equal rights and especially for equal opportunities in this
century? Perhaps it can be called a by-product of the current technological revolution. Some even label it oversimply a television revolution. Others speak of white realization that the increasingly interde-
pendent world is populated largely by nonwhite peoples. In reality,
the development is quite complicated.

Through the Model "T" Ford, other inexpensive transportation, and
the growing network of Southern roads came news of the tempting
outside world and labor contractors to hire Negroes for World War I
industries. They also made escape to a Northern "Paradise Valley" all
the easier as well as more tempting. Even the inadequate segregated
schools of the South were increasing Negro literacy; they joined with
the expansion of inexpensive picture newspapers and magazines to
broaden rural horizons.

As they became available, radio, tractors, chemical weed-killers,
mechanical cotton pickers, and television all converged to stimulate
new and bigger waves of migration to the urban ghettos in subsequent
decades. "Even though the weed-killers do not destroy weeds as
efficiently as hand-hoeing, they do permit the economies of tractor
use *and* mechanical pickers to be fully realized: this combination
sounded the death knell of the Negro hand-laborer."[18] Even as these
devices pushed Negroes from the Southern farms, radio and especially
television pulled him away by introducing him to the "American way
of life," how *every* American presumably should try to and be able to
live.

All these and other related developments helped to uproot poorly
educated rural Negroes in vast numbers and to confront them in
urban ghettos, in industrial plants, on union picket lines, in our armed
forces, and through television with the shocking contrasts between
America's advertised consumption goals and what they themselves
found they were able to attain. "In 1940, about three-fourths of all
nonwhites lived in the South and were largely engaged in agriculture.
By 1950, the proportion residing in the South had dropped to about
two-thirds, and today it is down to a little more than half. Even in the
South, nonwhites are now more concentrated in urban areas than ever
before."[19] In the whole country, Negro farm workers in 1950-66 declined from 18.4 to 6.1 percent of employed Negroes. This three to one
drop outran the little more than two to one decline (from 11.7 to 5.1
percent) in the employment of white workers on farms.[20]

At first glance, Northern financial opportunities for Negroes look good, especially in wartime. The urban-employed Negro's comparative economic lot did improve sharply from 1939 to 1948, but it has tended to settle downward again. Negro workers still earn less than two-thirds as much as white workers. A longer-time trend can be viewed by considering the lot in the American economy of the two tenths of the whole population with the lowest incomes, the portion containing a great many Negroes. By dividing the "spending units" of the United States into tenths in terms of their share of the national expendable personal income, it becomes clear that in 1910-37 the percentage received by the two lowest tenths declined by more than half (8.3 to 3.6) and that in 1937-65 they little more than held that proportion (about 4.0). In 1910, the two lowest tenths received about one-fourth of the share of the highest one tenth. In 1937, they received one-tenth as much, and in 1965, one-eighth. Negroes are disproportionately represented in the lower tenths and notably underrepresented in the top three tenths of the population.[21]

In this sketch of the general setting of racial tensions and disorders in this country, no extensive discussion is required of the omnipresence in the slums of interpersonal violence, of police pressures, of "prying" social workers with their needed but resented cash allotments, of prostitution, of gambling rackets, of dope and dope pushers, and of other types of delinquency and crime as ways of life. All these are familiar to the poverty-stricken—both white and colored. Many avoid involvement in them, but they do so only with great effort. All these problems can only be understood as parts of the whole setting outlined above. No one aspect of the whole situation, such as family disorganization,[22] can accurately be given special prominence as the determining factor. Both whites and Negroes, too, have a growing awareness of the significance of the nation's international situation in an overwhelmingly colored world.

Out of experiences with technological unemployment, with migration from farm to city and many times also from South to North, with picket lines in the Depression and in wartime, with training and combat and leisure-time activities in the armed forces, the Negroes of 1943 were ready to fight more effectively and more extensively than they had in past riots.

The riot pattern was not at all new. It had been evolving as American society evolved. In the 1943 Detroit outbreak, Negroes and whites spontaneously followed a riot pattern for which later both Negro and white leaders tried to find nonviolent alternatives. As nonviolent efforts led in many cases to impatience and disillusionment, the riot pattern continued to evolve. In its present form, it can now be seen in the frightening destructions of the mid-1960's.

What is the evolving riot pattern? The eighth chapter of the present book raises the questions: Did the same things happen in Los Angeles and Harlem as in Detroit? Is there a riot pattern? We realized that the more different riots we might compare, the more vague and the more general the similarities among them would be likely to become. The 1943 pattern we offer on pages 102 to 104 has, however, a transitional character between that of the riots of the World War I period and that of the 1960's. After all, we are dealing with an aspect of social process, of social history. In the relativity of social process, all things change, and so does the riot pattern. Even developments which appear to be the same at first glance have different contexts and tonalities. White raids and assaults of a more unilateral sort gave way to more of an interracial pattern of struggle and then to Negro rebellions.[23] From all the tensions, conflicts, and debates, too, there emerged more and more developed ideologies[24] of the changing Negro-white situation and of what Negroes and whites might do to improve it.

As the Negro writer Bayard Rustin[25] contends, perhaps the term "race riot" applied well enough to the Detroit riot of 1943 but has by the 1960's become "unilluminating and anchronistic." As he outlines the Detroit riot, "White mobs invaded the ghetto. Negroes forayed downtown. Men were beaten and murdered for the color of their skins." In the riots of 1964-67, on the other hand, "destruction has been confined to the ghetto; nor, discounting the police, were black and white citizens fighting. In fact, in Detroit [in 1967] whites joined in the looting and sniping. And I am told that whites were free to walk through the embattled ghetto without fear of violence from Negroes." As another journalist[26] put it, "Negro and white looters roved and thieved in integrated bands."

Reports of racist statements and acts by police and talk about "honkeys" and "whiteys," white exploitation, and white domination by Negroes make one vividly aware of the continuing interracial character of the conflicts. The struggles have tended to become more Negro reprisals against symbols or instruments of white power than riots between black and white mobs. Stated otherwise, Negro rioters

now fight chiefly against police who conceive of themselves as representatives of "the whole community" but are regarded by Negroes as
mercenaries of the white establishment. The riots of the 1960's have
become even more than fights by blacks against white exploitation
and domination; slum-dwellers regardless of color are starting to make
common cause in the struggles.

Let us re-examine, step by step, in a somewhat modified form, the
pattern we set forth in the eighth chapter of what *may* happen and
often has happened in a race riot. Into this, we integrate points made
there with regard to the character of the riot mob and its leaders, the
aftermath of a riot, its probable consequences, and preventive measures. In re-examining these steps, data available concerning the riots
of the 1960's as well as those of earlier decades will be compared with
the Detroit experiences of 1943 under these headings: (1) the makings
of a riot, (2) the triggering event, (3) crowd formation, (4) milling
and rumoring, (5) leadership emergence, (6) spread of the action,
(7) the army steps in, (8) exhaustion, (9) aftermath, and (10) consequences. Here, then, are the steps:

1. *The Makings of a Riot*

Behind each race riot is a rising tide of interracial irritation and
frustration stimulated by economic deprivation, political powerlessness, merchants' sharp practices, police arrogance, and incidents in
streets, parks, and mass transportation facilities. The sociologist Elliott
M. Rudwick[28] summarizes the background of the 1917 East St. Louis,
1919 Chicago, and 1943 Detroit riots as being: "threats to the security
of whites brought on by the Negroes' gains in economic, political, and
social status; Negro resentment of the attempts to 'kick him back into
his place'; and the weakness of the 'external forces of constraint'—the
city government, especially the police department."

In our estimation, Rudwick misplaces the significance of the "external forces of constraint." Our society joined in the development of
the situation existing in our Negro ghettos. It did so with the constant
and growing aid of police pressure and violence. The more exploitative and domineering the situation became and the more conscious
the dominated of their powerlessness to gain relief through legitimate
channels, the greater became the likelihood that they would use illegal
recourses. Vice and crime, often facilitated exploitatively by white

police and merchants, could only meet certain types of deprivation and those quite frustratingly.

Regardless of the strength of the "external forces of constraint," the policeman is confronted with what James Baldwin[29] calls "the silent, accumulating contempt and hatred of a people . . . like an occupying soldier in a bitterly hostile country, which is precisely what, and where, he is." As a sociological student[30] of the police notes, "Only when conditions vastly improve will Negroes be satisfied to test the sincerity of the white establishment by officially reporting cases of alleged police brutality, and then waiting for the scales of justice to balance." Until then, as he adds, "the police, as a symbol of white oppression, make an arrest at their peril. Riot remains a threat. Rebuffed by white society, the Negro community accepts its alienation as a virtue, and in turn rejects the legal channels of protest." As Brooklyn's militant Negro leader, the Rev. Milton Galamison,[31] asserted on a recent WABC press conference: "My answer is if one can't gain objectives through mediation around the table, if one can't gain objectives through peaceful demonstrations and picketing, if one can't even gain objectives after a riot, then all these things may become a Sunday School picnic by comparison to what people are going to do in order to get their just grievances remedied."

Our news-and-propaganda-and-entertainment organs explain to us quite plausibly how a foreign police state becomes constantly more repressive as it becomes constantly more dependent upon the use of force. It is as if force is a dike erected to confine a rising tide. The tide continues to rise, and the dike has to be made higher and higher and thus to become more and more precarious. Eventually the tide breaks through. We need to be more clear-eyed about the extent to which ghetto Negroes and city police are caught up in the same sort of police state situation. "External forces of constraint" may be thought to buy time, but they do so at a great and perhaps a disastrous cost. They will not solve a city's or a country's interracial problems. As a journalistic commentator[32] observes, "But how many members of the American press have gone beyond spot-news reporting with an all-out, continuing, comprehensive effort to help Americans understand ghetto conditions and ghetto desperation? How many of their staff members have exposed themselves to experiences which would help them understand? Here, indeed, is one of the major racial news gaps. . . . Two reporters for the Los Angeles *Times* won a Pulitzer Prize for a series on Watts, for example—but the series was commissioned *after* the Watts riot. Where was reporting of comparable length and depth before?"

As we point out in chapter nine, informed students of the Detroit interracial situation had predicted in advance that "race riots were inevitable."[33] *Life* magazine, July 28, 1967, spoke of the Newark rebellion as "The Predictable Insurrection." Somehow, civic, governmental, and business leaders have to learn what perceptive reporters and social scientists know about our interracial situation, or our makings of riots will continue to be "turned on" time and again in city after city.

2. *The Triggering Incident*

The event on the Belle Isle bridge which apparently precipitated the 1943 Detroit riot was mythical even though the rioting certainly got under way there at about the time the myth suggested. We mention several—both white and Negro—versions of this myth in chapter three. That the myth was widely told and believed and fitted so plausibly into the crescendo of tension and violence was enough to turn the makings of a riot into an actual one.[34]

The transformation stemming from a triggering incident is shockingly dramatic. Up to that point, hatreds and irritations are either confined, held within bounds by a sense of social pressures, or expressed in interpersonal bickerings or conflicts. The triggering incident becomes a declaration of war. Suddenly, as it were, the rules are changed. All those who feel sufficiently desperate—whether members of a mob or of the police—find a permissible and jointly protected outlet for their welled-up frustrations. What had been interpersonal becomes intergroup.

The triggering event 24 years later in Detroit was called by *Newsweek*[35] "the classic one: a trivial police incident." Here are details:

> On teeming Twelfth Street, . . . police mounted a routine 4 a.m. raid on a 'blind pig'—an after-hours speakeasy in an abandoned second-floor office. The weather was muggy, the street tense; hours earlier two carloads of Negroes had coursed through whooping, 'Unite, black men! This is a stand! Black power!' As the blue raiders flushed 80 captives downstairs, knots of Negroes materialized outside, jeering at first, then tossing rocks and bricks at the cops. A brick smashed a cruiser window—a direct hit that turned out to be the declaration of war.

The study of 76 race riots in 1913-63, cited above,[36] concludes that "precipitating incidents often involve highly charged offenses committed by members of one group against the other, such as attacks on women, police brutality and interference, murder, and assault. In recent years, violation of segregation taboos by Negroes as well as white resistance have been increasingly frequent precipitants."

To a degree, the character of the precipitating incident symptomizes the type of riot that follows. The 1943 Detroit incident involved either white or black mob action, and the subsequent rioting included many actions by aggressive mobs. The 1943 Harlem incident centered on a police action, and the subsequent rioting had the character of a Negro uprising against police and merchants as symbols of white domination.

3. Crowd Formation

During the period when the makings of a riot still lack the incendiary spark of a triggering incident, much can be done to divert a city from a racial "collision course." In retrospect, however, controversy often focuses upon how the precipitating event might have been so handled by the police as to make it just another in a long series of limited, interpersonal conflicts. To illustrate, Newsweek[37] contended that "at the flash point" in the 1967 Detroit riot, "police made the first in a series of fateful mistakes. They might have pulled out in the hope the crowd would disperse—or they could have moved forward in full force to nip the trouble in the bud." They did neither. They merely paraded cruisers in order to overawe the mob, and the "war . . . quickly escalated." It is unlikely that either of Newsweek's alternatives would have stopped the riot. Too much tinder had collected. It was too widely scattered throughout the deprived areas of the city. And it had already started to flash into flames. In spite of all that the city government, with Federal aid, had tried to do to improve the Negro's situation, centuries of repression require even more than heroic efforts at amelioration. We are learning that we are in a social revolution, and a social revolution requires drastic and painful adaptations if it is not to be a bloody one.

The English social scientist E. J. Hobsbawm[38] defined a mob "as the movement of all classes of the urban poor for the achievement of economic or political changes by direct action—that is by riot or rebellion—but as a movement which was as yet inspired by no specific ideology. . . . It was a 'pre-political' movement." Even though he was writing in 1959, Hobsbawm appeared to feel secure in noting the mob's "passing" as a social phenomenon. If he had been better acquainted with the affairs of such countries as the United States of America and India, to mention but two, he could not have come to such a conclusion. At any rate, his other points about a mob approximate well enough those in an American race riot. The sociologist Herbert Blumer[39] adds the practical comment, "To prevent the formation of a mob or to break up a mob it is necessary to redirect the attention so that it is not focused collectively on one object." The polarization of a race riot mob is very great. It is deeply ingrained in ancient usage, and it is intense. Reports of riot after riot suggest that the mobs involved are more likely to disperse through eventual exhaustion than through diversion, but diversion might well be tried.

The crowd gathers in response to the triggering incident. It starts very quickly to act. It becomes a mob. It furnishes the media through which hysterical, inciting rumors travel. Other mobs form in other parts of the city. In spite of recurrent riots in such cities as Detroit and New York, both white and black police as contributors to the makings of riots are scarcely prepared to cope with such outbreaks. In city after city, as in the cases described in this book, the police figured as participants rather than as mediators or inhibitors or purveyors of "one of the most humane services a human being can render to his fellows," to quote a textbook for policemen.[40] Thus something of the mob spirit also infects the police, in part in consequence of their being cast in the roles of participants by ghetto dwellers.

4. Milling and Rumoring

Milling and rumoring are processes through which acting crowds or mobs and, in a more guarded way, police and government officials build morale and esprit de corps for hazardous conflict. As Blumer[41] outlines it, "In milling, individuals move around amongst one another in an aimless and random fashion . . . in a state of excitement. The primary effect of milling is to make the individuals more sensitive and responsive to one another . . . much more disposed to act together, under the influence of a common impulse or mood." They also push the more susceptible members of the mob on towards overt acts of violence, acts those pushing are themselves not ready to undertake but are willing to help sponsor. Those pushed are typically the younger, the more crime-prone, the more disturbed mentally. They serve as shock troops for a mob.

Rumors are "attempts by confused individuals to comprehend ambiguous situations by filling gaps in their knowledge."[42] Even when factually inaccurate, as rumors so often are, at least in detail, they usually contribute to the conflict pattern. They provide justification apparently needed at the time for a course of action then in process. They are part of a mob's morale-building interactions.

5. Leadership Emergence

Our outline on page 103 of the degrees of participation in a race riot mob summarize general American experience since the riots of the World War I period. We still have (1) young leaders (the most excited and violent mobsters, the ones whom the rank-and-file emulate); (2) older leaders (vicious middle-aged hoodlums or natural leaders who believe that the incident beginning the riot endangers "their people," "their homes," "their safety"); (3) rank-and-file rioters, who participate but not on the fervid scale of the young leaders; and (4) bystanders, who enjoy vicariously but emphatically the emotional "jag" of being a part of the "show" without taking the risk of doing any of the fighting or other activities of a dangerous sort.

Whites and blacks who are involved in the status quo typically try to buy "another chance" during a riot through giving carte blanche to their specialists in physical force, the police, about whose attitudes and activities civic, governmental, and business leaders as well as professional people know little of an accurate or comprehensive sort. Thus, the top leadership of respectable Negro organizations—Roy Wilkins of the National Association for the Advancement of Colored People, Whitney Young of the Urban League, the Rev. Martin Luther King, Jr., and A. Philip Randolph, the union leader—jointly signed a statement following the 1967 Detroit riot asserting: "Killing, arson, looting are criminal acts and should be dealt with as such. . . . We are confident that the overwhelming majority of the Negro community joins us in opposition to violence in the streets."[43] But time has passed their rhetoric by. Negroes had found an instrument for the dramatization of their dissatisfactions which the white establishment could not easily brush aside. Rather than police action against criminal acts, perhaps something closer to a peace conference with rebel leaders in city after city is becoming the indicated recourse. It would have been a foresighted course during or following the Detroit riots of 1925 or 1943 or 1967. Meanwhile, slum rioters continue to develop daring leaders, techniques of organization and strategy, materiel for combat, goals, and ideologies. Their "pre-political" stage, to use Hobsbawm's[38] term, may now be passing. Their "political" stage, growing out of centuries of bitterness, may be even more difficult for the white community to understand and to confront.

6. Spread of the Action

Mayor Jeffries, Police Commissioner Witherspoon, and County Prosecutor Dowling tried hard to pin the blame for the spread of the 1943 race riot on the Negro people. Overlooking the speedy development of other riot focal points by those leaving the Belle Isle rioting, Witherspoon and Dowling attempted to make the riot announcement in a Negro night club the major cause of the spread. As we outline it in chapter three of this book, rioting spread from the bridge almost immediately. War had been declared. The fever apparently had to run its disastrous course.

In the 1943 Harlem riot, as we indicate, skilful police leadership aided by the heads of Negro and trade union bodies confined the rioting to a limited area, but in other major riots this has rarely been the case. The whole Negro ghetto typically becomes involved before tensions expressed in violence start to ebb. The speed of spread has made many contend that our major riots were planned, but there appears to be little evidence of such guidance. What has happened in our riots can quite adequately be explained in terms of largely spontaneous activities.

The Federal Bureau of Investigation[44] published an analysis of the seven major city race riots of 1964 in which special attention was given to allegations of instigation. The report asserts: "These charges have been carefully investigated. The evidence indicates that aside from the actions of minor organizations or irresponsible individuals there was no systematic planning or organization of any of the city riots."

7. *The Army Steps in*

Few cities employ a police force sufficiently large for it to be drained
to a riot area and speedily suppress a major turbulence. A great many
mayors are thus driven very quickly to cry for one or more of the
three possible additional waves of organized physical pressure—(2)
the state police, (3) the state national guards, and (4) the Federal
troops. State police differ from the local chiefly through being more
disciplined, cohesive, and mobile; possibly they are also more objective through being less directly involved in local affairs. The prejudices
of individual state policemen are likely to be similar to those of their
city brethren, but they are also more likely to do as ordered. The
part-time soldiers of the national guard units, when mobilized for riot
duty, have shown themselves to be poorly disciplined and even more
prejudiced than local and state police in identifying themselves with
white control interests, as they understand them. On the other hand,
experienced Federal troops—on the rare occasions that they have been
used—have brought the most exemplary degree of objectivity to riot
control.

The extent of the prejudice, mob-like thinking, and even terror local
police can generate in themselves is well illustrated by several incidents. During the 1943 Detroit riot, the Rev. Horace J. White, pastor
of the city's largest Negro Protestant church, volunteered to enlist 200
auxiliaries. Police Commissioner Witherspoon agreed to the idea. When
White's volunteers as a crowd were going down Beaubien Street, the
police assumed they were about to be overwhelmed and prepared for
battle. Fortunately they got "the word" before they fired a shot. The
Negroes were only used in a limited manner. In Newark's 1967 riot,
"a Negro policeman in civilian clothes was beaten by white policemen
when he tentered the Fourth Precinct to report for duty."[45] As a
young Negro, killed by a policeman a few minutes later, told a *Life*[46]
reporter: "We ain't riotin' agains' all you whites. We're riotin' agains'
police brutality, like that cab driver they beat up the other night [the
triggering incident of the 1967 Newark riot]. That stuff goes on all the
time. When the police treat us like people 'stead of treatin' us like
animals, then the riots will stop."

In the 1967 Detroit riot, the national guardsmen "proved to be, as
they had in Watts and Newark, a ragged, jittery, hair-triggered lot ill-
trained in riot control." One young guardsman, "hand trembling on the

butt of his M-1 rifle, growled, 'I'm gonna shoot anything that moves and is black.' Some of his comrades in arms seemed to do precisely that. Tanks strafed buildings indiscriminately in the hunt for snipers. The death toll spiraled."[47] On the contrary, when the Federal troops finally got into Detroit and took over control of half of the riot zone, they "packed only small arms . . . and steady trigger fingers. While the guard's machine guns chopped randomly at building fronts, the paratroopers isolated real snipers' nests, stalked them with deadly, dogged accuracy and quickly pacified the East Side."[48]

The Federal troops stopped the 1943 Detroit riot. If they had been sufficiently numerous and had taken over control of the whole fourteen square miles of the riot area in 1967, they would have stopped that one as promptly as they were permitted by political jostling to arrive. As it was, they helped to confine it "to Detroit's poorest, angriest surviving ghetto at the city's center, and it took on the chilling cast of guerilla warfare."[49]

While we do not believe that armed intervention should ever be regarded as accomplishing anything other than buying some time, we advised in this book and elsewhere and still believe, "Should a race riot break out, make sure that the . . . U.S. Army is on its way as soon as the danger becomes apparent."[50] In view of what we have learned from reports on a hundred or so subsequent race riots, we have deleted the words, "the state militia and." Only well-trained state police and Federal troops are likely to be helpful and then only, we repeat, in buying time.

8. Exhaustion

The riots reported in this book were apparently stopped, but a great many major riots terminate through exhaustion rather than effective strategy. "In the end," *Newsweek* reported August 7, 1967, "the [Detroit] riot burned itself out. By the weekend, the curfew had been lifted once, then reimposed as a check not on snipers but on sightseers."

The three thousand national guardsmen New Jersey's governor sent into Newark in 1967 apparently prolonged that riot. "By Sunday the crisis was nearing a new stage. If the occupation [by state troops] of Friday and Saturday was going to continue, the community would have started to counterattack in a real way. 'Why should we quit,' one kid wanted to know, 'when they got twenty-five of us and only two of them are dead?' "[51] If the state troops had not created a new conflict situation, a new sense of threat to the Negro community, exhaustion might have terminated the riot without the taking of so many as twenty more lives, the toll of the guardsmen.

9. Aftermath

If we had not talked with a great many whites and Negroes after the 1943 Detroit and Harlem riots, we could not have brought ourselves to write as we did about the chief characteristics of a riot's aftermath. The "veterans" of both sides are proud of the outcome. Both whites and Negroes can easily still any possible guilt feelings at their participation in violence; they feel no more guilty than soldiers who have fought for "God, country, and hearth." Both sides, too, react with a kind of team spirit to the possibility of a "return engagement." The police turn to the development of more effective repressive measures, with some side glances at human relations amenities.[52] Negroes find themselves driven to thinking in terms of community-protective devices. Negro extremists try to offer to the Negro community the sort of protection police offer to the whites. Similarities between this tactic of Negro extremists and that of the Nazis and Fascists in Germany and Italy are not far-fetched. How far they might get depends upon the extent to which our governmental and other leaders gain the confidence of the Negroes. As middle-class Negroes become more and more bound in again to the Negro community, and isolated and disillusioned with white leaders, the road to reconciliation has become a long and difficult one.

10. Consequences

Other white students[53] of the 1943 Detroit race riot contended recently, "A look over the last twenty years or so makes clear that race riots paralyze efforts to attack racial problems." In so saying, they touch upon one of the most crucial aspects of the social debate over the consequences of race riots, but they at the same time are apparently blind to the social roles of race riots. A cogent Negro journalist[54] sees the "riotous summer of 1943 [as] . . . a basic turning point in the Negro-white dialogue. The riots of that year illuminated the outstanding debts and the outstanding hatreds. Fearful of similar explosions, cities all over America 'discovered' the race problem. By 1945, more than four hundred committees, official and unofficial, had been established by American communities." Interest in racial inequities then subsided not because of the 1943 riots but because the urgency of the Negro's needs appeared to subside. As Elmo Ellis,[55] general manager of radio station WSB, Atlanta, Georgia, has asserted, "Riots are ugly, but they are not meaningless. They cry out profoundly for understanding and corrective action."

What can be done about this "new, militant voice from the ghetto . . . a harsh voice, impolite, unpredictable, certainly not always controllable?" For all the denunciations of "black power," those who have studied our depressed groups most carefully know that "a piece of power . . . is what the ghetto needs most."[56] But what about specifics? What can this lead to? When a journalist[57] recently asked Floyd McKissick, head of the Congress of Racial Equality (CORE), what the black man now wanted, he "turned and fixed his questioner with a flat, unsmiling stare. 'The answer is everything *you* got right now, and everything you hope to get.' " If a white immigrant had said that, it would have been taken as an expression of the kind of aspiration a good American should have. Why should it sound ominous when it comes from a Negro? His folks have been here a lot longer, on the average, than all other Americans except the Indians.

REFERENCES

1. Quoted by Lerone Bennett, Jr., *Confrontation* (New York: Pelican Books, 1966), p. 9.

2. *Op.cit.*, p. 11. See also A. McC. Lee, *Multivalent Man* (New York: George Braziller, 1966), esp. chaps. 1-3.

3. M. J. Herskovits, "Ancestry of the American Negro," *Opportunity, 17* (1939): 22-23, 27-31, at p. 30.

4. Herbert Aptheker, *American Negro Slave Revolts* (New York: Columbia University Press, 1943).

5. Maurice Rea Davie, *Negroes in American Society* (New York: McGraw-Hill Book Co., 1949), p. 45.

6. *Ibid.*, p. 54.

7. J. E. Cutler, *Lynch-law* (New York: Longmans, Green & Co., 1905); A. F. Raper, *The Tragedy of Lynching* (Chapel Hill: University of

North Carolina Press, 1933); Gunnar Myrdal, Richard Sterner, and A. M. Rose, *An American Dilemma* (New York: Harper & Brothers, 1944), chap. 27.

8. Stanley Lieberson and A. R. Silverman, "The Precipitants and Under-lying Conditions of Race Riots," *American Sociological Review, 30* (1965): 887-898, esp. pp. 887-889.

9. E. M. Rudwick, *Race Riot at East St. Louis July 2, 1917* (Carbondale: Southern Illinois University Press, 1964).

10. Chicago Commission on Race Relations, *The Negro in Chicago* (Chicago: University of Chicago Press, 1922). Prepared under the direction of G. R. Taylor and C. S. Johnson.

11. Myrdal, *op. cit.*, pp. 568-569.

12. Rudwick, *op. cit.*, p. 233.

13. Quoted in "The Racial Crisis: A Consensus," *Newsweek*, August 21, 1967, pp. 16-22, 25-26, at p. 25.

14. Quoted in *ibid.*

15. "The Old South Had Something Worth Saving," New York *Times Magazine*, December 4, 1966, pp. 50-51, 170, 172, 174, 176-177, 179, at p. 51.

16. C. M. Melden, *From Slave to Citizen* (New York: Methodist Book Concern, 1921), p. 147.

17. Quoted by J. A. Lukas, "Postscript on Detroit: 'Whitey Hasn't Got the Message,'" New York *Times Magazine*, August 27, 1967, pp. 24-25, 43, 46, 48, 51, 53, 56, 58, at p. 43.

18. H. C. Dillingham and D. F. Sly, "The Mechanical Cotton-Picker, Negro Migration, and the Integration Movement," *Human Organization, 25* (1966): 344-351, at p. 346.

19. H. P. Miller, "The Distribution of Personal Income in the United States," chap. 42 in D. H. Wrong and H. L. Gracey, eds., *Introductory Sociology* (New York: Macmillan Co., 1967), at p. 455. See also Miller, *Rich Man, Poor Man* (New York: T. Y. Crowell Co., 1964).

20. Reports, Dept. of Labor, Bureau of Labor Statistics.

21. Gabriel Kolko, *Wealth and Power in America* (New York: Frederick A. Praeger, 1962), pp. 14-15, and University of Michigan, Survey Research Center, *Survey of Consumer Finances*, through 1965.

22. D. P. Moynihan, "Employment, Income, and the Ordeal of the Negro Family," *Daedalus, 94* (1965): 745-770. See also "The Moynihan Report": *The Negro Family: The Case for National Action* (Office of

Policy Planning and Research, U.S. Dept. of Labor, March, 1965).

23. H. O. Dahlke, "Race and Minority Riots—A Study in the Typology of Violence," *Social Forces, 30* (1952): 419-425; A. D. Grimshaw, "Factors Contributing to Colour Violence in the United States and Britain," *Race, 3* (1962): 3-19, "Three Major Cases of Colour Violence in the United States," *Race, 5* (1963): 76-86, and "Urban Racial Violence in the United States," *American Journal of Sociology, 66* (1960): 109-119; and Lieberson and Silverman, *op. cit.*: esp. pp. 897-898.

24. A. McC. Lee, "Il persistere delle ideologie," *La Critica Sociologica, 1* (Roma, 1967): 5-15.

25. "A Way Out of the Exploding Ghetto," New York *Times Magazine,* August 13, 1967, pp. 16-17, 54, 59-60, 62, 64-65, at p. 17.

26. E. J. Hughes, "The Great Disgrace," *Newsweek,* August 7, 1967, p. 17.

27. F. C. Shapiro and J. W. Sullivan, *Race Riots: New York 1964* (New York: T. Y. Crowell Co., 1964); Tom Hayden, *Rebellion in Newark* (New York: Vintage Books, 1967); R. C. Maynard, "The Black Revolt," New York *Post,* September 25, 1967 *et seq.*

28. *Op. cit.,* p. 217.

29. "Fifth Avenue, Uptown," pp. 346-355 in Eric and Mary Josephson, eds., *Man Alone* (New York: Dell Publishing Co., 1962), at pp. 352-353.

30. Arthur Niederhoffer, *Behind the Shield: The Police in Urban Society* (Garden City, N.Y.: Doubleday & Co., 1967), pp. 183-184.

31. Quoted by Shapiro and Sullivan, *op. cit.,* pp. 207-208.

32. Alfred Balk, "The Racial News Gap," *Saturday Review,* August 13, 1966, pp. 53-54, at p. 53.

33. Detroit *Free Press,* June 22, 1943.

34. Tamotsu Shibutani, *Improvised News: A Sociological Study of Rumor* (Indianapolis: Bobbs-Merrill Co., 1966), esp. chap. 6.

35. August 7, 1967, p. 19.

36. Lieberson and Silverman, *op. cit.,* pp. 896-897.

37. August 7, 1967, p. 19.

38. *Primitive Rebels* (New York: F. A. Praeger, 1959), pp. 110, 124. See esp. chap. 7, "The City Mob."

39. "Collective Behavior," part 4 of A. McC. Lee, ed., *Principles of Sociology,* 2nd ed. rev. (New York: Barnes & Noble, 1966), p. 181.

40. A. C. Germann, F. D. Day, and R. R. J. Gallati, *Introduction to Law Enforcement* (Springfield, Ill.: C. C. Thomas, 1962), p. 186.

41. *Op. cit.*, p. 174.

42. Shibutani, *op. cit.*, p. 163.

43. *Newsweek*, August 7, 1967, p. 25.

44. *Report*, September 18, 1964, 10 pp., at p. 5.

45. Hayden, *op. cit.*, p. 19.

46. Dale Wittner, "The Killing of Billy Furr," *Life*, July 28, 1967, pp. 20-23, at p. 21.

47. "An American Tragedy, 1967—Detroit," *Newsweek*, August 7, 1967, pp. 18-26, at p. 20.

48. *Ibid.*

49. *Ibid.*

50. A. McC. Lee, *Race Riots Aren't Necessary* (New York: Public Affairs Committee), 1945, p. 29.

51. Hayden, *op. cit.*, p. 60.

52. G. P. McManus, "Practical Measures for Police Control of Riots and Mobs," *FBI Law Enforcement Bulletin*, October 1962; E. W. Purdy, "Riot Control—A Local Responsibility," *FBI Law Enforcement Bulletin*, June 1965; Rex Applegate, *Crowd and Riot Control* (Harrisburg, Pa.: Stackpole Co., 1965).

53. Robert Shogan and Tom Craig, *The Detroit Race Riot* (Philadelphia: Chilton Books, 1964), p. 142.

54. Bennett, *op. cit.*, p. 160.

55. Quoted by S. G. Davis and W. N. Schultz, "Riot Coverage: Cool it?" *The Quill*, October 1967, pp. 16-20, at p. 20.

56. Bernard Asbell, "Dick Lee Discovers How Much Is Enough," New York *Times Magazine*, September 3, 1967, pp. 6-7, 31, 40-42, at p. 42.

57. F. C. Shapiro, "The Successor to Floyd McKissick May Not Be So Reasonable," New York *Times Magazine*, October 1, 1967, pp. 32-33, 98-105, at p. 105.

ADDITIONAL RECOMMENDED READINGS

Barron, Milton L., ed., *Minorities in a Changing World* (New York: Alfred A. Knopf, 1967), esp. parts V and VII.

Brink, William, and Louis Harris, *Black and White: A Study of U.S. Racial Attitudes Today* (New York: Simon and Schuster, 1967).

Brown, Claude, *Manchild in the Promised Land* (New York: Macmillan Co., 1965).

Carmichael, Stokely, and C. V. Hamilton, *Black Power: The Politics of Liberation in America* (New York: Random House, 1967).

Clark, Kenneth B., *Dark Ghetto: Dilemmas of Social Power* (New York: Harper & Row, 1965).

Cohen, Jerry, and William S. Murphy, *Burn, Baby, Burn! The Los Angeles Race Riot, August 1965* (New York: Avon Book, 1966).

Conot, Robert, *Rivers of Blood, Years of Darkness* (New York: Bantam Books, 1967).

Donnan, Elizabeth, ed., *Documents Illustrative of the History of the Slave Trade to America* (New York: Octagon Books, 1965), 4 vols.

Elliott, Osborn, ed., "The Negro in America: What Must Be Done," *Newsweek*, November 20, 1967, pp. 32-42, 46-48, 51-54, 57-60, 65.

Franklin, John Hope, *From Slavery to Freedom* (New York: Alfred A. Knopf, 1956).

Kozol, Jonathan, *Death at an Early Age: The Destruction of the Hearts and Minds of Negro Children in the Boston Public Schools* (Boston: Houghton Mifflin Co., 1967).

Lewis, Hylan, *Culture, Class and Poverty* (Washington: CROSSTELL, February, 1967).

Liebow, Elliot, *Tally's Corner: A Study of Negro Streetcorner Men* (Boston: Little, Brown and Co., 1967).

Oxaal, Ivar, *Black Intellectuals Come to Power* (Cambridge: Schenkman Publishing Co., 1967).

Pettigrew, Thomas F., *A Profile of the Negro American* (Princeton: D. Van Nostrand Co., 1964).

Rainwater, Lee, William L. Yancey, and others. *The Moynihan Report and the Politics of Controversy* (Cambridge: The M.I.T. Press, 1967).

Rose, Peter I., *They and We* (New York: Random House, 1964).

ACKNOWLEDGMENTS

THE facts in this report are based upon the authors' own first-hand observations of the 1943 Detroit race riots and, in addition, upon a number of helpful sources, the aid of which is hereby gratefully acknowledged.

The three general-circulation daily newspapers of Detroit—the morning *Free Press* and the evening *News* and *Times*—carried detailed and useful accounts of events, official statements, and official actions throughout the period. The Negro weeklies, the *Michigan Chronicle* and Detroit *Tribune*, and the monthly *Racial Digest*, supplied similarly helpful material. Additional facts, interpretations, and sidelights were obtained from *The Detroiter* (Detroit Board of Commerce), Detroit *Labor News, Michigan C.I.O. News*, New York *Times*, New York *PM*, New York *Post*, *The New Republic, Life*, and *Time*.

Our students in sociology at Wayne University furnished us with observations and emotional reactions of a wide range of Negro and white citizens throughout Detroit, and, as will be seen in the text, their contributions are of especial value. Among these many students, we wish to thank particularly the following: Gertrude Atyeo, Gloria Bradford, Mabel Carpenter, Eugene Dewandeler, Jesse DeWitt, Virginia Durand, Betty Elliott, Larry Finkel, Dorr Fockler, John Fuko, C. E. Hutchinson, Frieda Smolinsky Leman, Grace E. Lints, James McKeown, Margaret Pyle, Norman Rosenberg, Kathryn Rosenberg, Kathryn Schultz, Nellie Shinn, Ruth Smith, Crescence Wagner, and Ida Younglove.

Our colleagues in sociology, Professors Edward C. Jandy, Maude Fiero, Donald C. Marsh, and H. Warren Dunham, were also most cooperative in cordially giving us the benefit of their suggestions and observations. Clarence Anderson, Executive Secretary, Metropolitan Detroit Fair Employment Practice Committee (a Detroit War Chest activity), gave unstintingly of his observations and insights. Rosina Mohaupt, Research Assistant, Detroit Bureau of Governmental Research, kindly provided us with valuable map materials. Prof. Curtis D. MacDougall, Northwestern University; Dr. Norman F. Kinzie, Director of Social Service, Detroit Council of Churches; his secretary, Bertha Cook; and Frank E. Hartung, Detroit Civil Service Commission, helped us to obtain otherwise unavailable information. Walter White, Secretary, National Association for the Advancement of Colored People; Dr. John W. Riley, Jr., Dept. of Sociology, Rutgers University; and William H. Baldwin, President, National Urban League, kindly made available to us results of their own first-hand observations and investigations in Detroit. The foregoing also read parts or all of the manuscript and made constructive suggestions and criticisms.

The following kindly aided us in many ways, especially in suggestions, comments, and criticisms of the first draft of this book:

Philip A. Adler, Columnist, Detroit *News*

Dr. Thoburn T. Brumbaugh, Secretary, Detroit Council of Churches

Dr. Stanley Hastings Chapman, Dept. of Sociology, University of Pennsylvania

Hon. George Edwards, Member, Detroit City Council

Isaac Franck, Executive Director, Jewish Community Council of Detroit

Prof. E. Franklin Frazier, Dept. of Sociology, Howard University

Msgr. Francis J. Haas, Chairman, U. S. Fair Employment Practice Committee

Raymond O. Hatcher, Group Work Secretary, Detroit Urban League

Helen F. Humphrey, Attorney-at-Law, Washington, D. C.

Prof. Charles S. Johnson, Dept. of Sociology, Fisk University

Dr. F. Ernest Johnson, Executive Secretary, Dept. of Research and Education, Federal Council of the Churches of Christ in America

W. K. Kelsey, "The Commentator," Detroit *News*

Dr. George Hamor Lee, Dept. of Applied Mechanics, Cornell University

Dr. James J. McClendon, President, Detroit Chapter, National Association for the Advancement of Colored People

Saul Mills, Secretary-Treasurer, Greater New York Industrial Union Council

Prof. E. B. Reuter, Dept. of Sociology, University of Iowa

Prof. Charles Shull, Dept. of Government, Wayne University

Shelton Tappes, Recording Secretary, Local 600, United Automobile Workers of America (C.I.O.)

R. J. Thomas, President, United Automobile Workers of America (C.I.O.)

Mrs. Beulah T. Whitby, Director, Emergency Relief Division, Office of Civilian Defense, Detroit

Rev. Horace White, Plymouth Congregational Church, Detroit

Rev. Claude Williams, Institute of Applied Religion and the Detroit Presbytery

Particularly helpful in this undertaking were Stanley Burnshaw and Donald Ambler, executives of The Dryden Press. They aided in the development of the outline and ideas of the book and made many worthwhile suggestions, both editorial and analytical. Prof. Willard Waller of Columbia University, Prof. Maurice R. Davie of Yale University, and Irving D. Robbins of the Institute of Public Relations suggested ideas and made critical comments of great value. And finally we wish to mention the patience and understanding with which our wives, Dr. Elizabeth Briant Lee and Elizabeth Roos Humphrey, co-operated in this venture.

Naturally, the authors jointly assume full responsibility for the facts and conclusions as set forth in the finished product, but the book would have been impossible had it not actually been the joint enterprise of many people.

Thirty-four Americans died in the Detroit race riots of the week of June 20, 1943. They died while their relatives were fighting in American uniforms on the battlefields of a war for freedom. It is sincerely hoped that this book points to a few of the lessons we Americans must learn from this hysterical attack upon democracy and American morale.

A. McC. L.

N. D. H.

Wayne University
Detroit, Michigan
September, 1943

CONTENTS

I. WHAT CAUSES RACE RIOTS?

Chapter 1

WHY DO PEOPLE RIOT?
AN OPENING GLIMPSE

THIRTY-FOUR Americans died and more than one thousand others were wounded in the streets of Detroit—in the heart of the "Arsenal of Democracy"—during Negro-white clashes the week of June 20, 1943. Their relatives were fighting and dying on battlefields thousands of miles away in a war for freedom, but the blood of these men and women on the home front was spilled in a senseless, hysterical race riot.

The responsible citizens of Detroit and America recoiled from a spectacle such as must have shocked the responsible people of Berlin and Rome during the early days of the Nazis and the Fascisti: Hate-ridden mobs streamed through the central business district, the nearby slums, and even City Hall square. They assaulted Negroes at will, derided policemen who were trying to restore a semblance of order, and brought admissions from the Mayor that the situation was out of control.

This is a picture of one part of the Land of the Free on Monday, June 21, 1943, in the midst of a global war fought for the Four Freedoms:

Shootings. Beatings. Looting. Property destruction. Car-burnings. Maimed and wounded innocents. A terrified populace. A horrified minority, inadequately protected and besieged in an American city.

Here are a few incidents of those bloody hours:

"Here's some *fresh meat!* Fresh meat, boys! The conductor's a nigger! C'mon. Fresh meat!"

The white drunk screamed these words. The mob converged on the moving streetcar. The motorman jammed on more power, and his car went crashing through the crowd. . . .

At another place, a white man with a crowbar stopped a streetcar and demanded, "Are there any niggers in there?" Then he broke down the door, and the mob dashed in. This is what a Negro in the car saw and heard and felt:

"The mob rushed into the car and passed me, going toward the back after other passengers. I jumped up and ran out.

"As I stepped from the car into the safety zone, three shots were fired at me. I felt pain in my right side and in my chest. I ran to where police were standing and said: 'Help me, I'm shot!'

"The officers took me to the middle of the street where they held me. I begged them not to let the rioters attack me. While they held me by both arms, nine or ten men walked out of the crowd and struck me hard blows.

"Men kept coming up to me and beating me, and the policemen did nothing to prevent it."

This Negro was Sam Mitchell, veteran of the Western Front in World War I. . . .

On another street, a white war-plant worker froze to the ground as a mob of Negro hoodlums surrounded him on his way home from work. Was this America, his adopted land? Wasn't his son in a Japanese prison camp, an American prisoner of war?

"Run home if you don't want to be killed," they told his women companions from the factory. Then they knocked him down, kicked him, and left him bleeding. John Holyak, 59, father of Private John Holyak, 36, who had been captured at Bataan, died five days later. . . .

How can this happen in America? What can America learn from Detroit? *What must America learn from Detroit?* Do riots follow a pattern? Can they be predicted? Are they engineered by subversive agents? Can they be prevented? Will there be more race riots in Detroit? Will the hated virus spread to other cities—to Chicago, Pittsburgh, Philadelphia, Washington, and elsewhere? Does it infect Los Angeles and New York?

Newspapermen, politicians, political scientists, psychiatrists, and sociologists have given a great deal of time and effort to the study of race differences, race hatreds, bigotry, intolerance, and riots. Have we arrived at any "answers" from such joint work that can help the United States fight more effectively against this vile and divisive threat to national morale?

"Fascist Attitude of Mind"

The "answers" of politicians are certainly not adequate. As Wendell L. Willkie put it on July 24, 1943, talking about the Detroit race riots, the attitudes of the two major political parties towards the Negro can be thought of in terms of "their separate ways of approaching the Negro vote." He then tells how one party "has a tendency to ask the Negro for his vote as recompense for an act of simple justice done eighty years ago." And he points out that the other party "retains political power by, in effect, depriving the Negro of his right to vote in one part of the country, while seeking his vote in another on the plea of great friendship for his race." Willkie attributed race riots in Detroit, Los Angeles, and Beaumont, Texas, to "the same basic motivation as actuates the fascist mind." He defines this "fascist attitude of mind" as the "desire to deprive some of our citizens of their rights—economic, civic or political"—and points out that it has "the same basic motivation as activates the fascist mind when it seeks to dominate whole peoples and nations."

Newspapermen, psychiatrists, and sociologists would agree more readily with Wendell L. Willkie than with the apparent attitudes of the two major parties, as expressed by their lesser figures—especially by their ward and district leaders. The terms of scientists might be different, but their theories would be similar. A few pages devoted to what psychiatrists and sociologists have learned in general about race clashes of this sort will help us understand the race riots in Detroit. And some of these thoughtful findings will enable us to see a little more clearly the pattern followed by the Detroit riots, when that pattern is outlined in detail in the second section of this book.

On "Losing Face"

When psychiatrists and sociologists start talking about why people riot, they turn immediately to several fundamental questions that lie beneath actual rioting. They ask: In their daily lives, what poses and claims and activities did the rioters use to give themselves distinction from their fellows and from people in general? What did they brag about? In what ways were these people recently frustrated in their efforts to get ego-gratifying satisfaction? In other words, who and what recently made them "lose face"?

These may sound like strange and all-too-homely starting points.

But riots—like wars, strikes, real estate sales, and engagements to be married—do not break into public notice without a long course of individual and social preparation. *Riots are the products of thousands upon thousands of little events that have affected the habits and emotions of thousands upon thousands of people, both future rioters and future innocent bystanders.*

What sociologists point to here is a simple truth discovered long ago by politicians, salesmen, and psychiatrists—and somewhat later by Dale Carnegie. This simple truth is that men and women find it highly necessary to give themselves a feeling of importance, a sense of distinction. They can accomplish this in many ways: They can belong to the gangs, unions, sewing circles, women's clubs, lodges, or luncheon clubs that they have learned to regard as important, as containing "real people." They can excel at being better machinists, fathers, mothers, humorists, drinkers, thieves, rabble-rousers, or "tough guys" than their fellows. They can glory in having the biggest or best family, stamp collection, house, physique, or stalk of corn in the district. They can establish to their own satisfaction their superiority to others through what is technically called ethnocentrism or group-egotism. They can do this by claiming a group exclusiveness or group destiny or group virtue based upon ancestry or racial superiority, and they can confirm this through joining the Sons of the American Revolution, the Ku Klux Klan, or the German-American Bund. The fact that many members are ignorant of the ideological principles of these organizations makes very little difference—to the ignorant ones or the leaders—so long as the group egotism is satisfied.

When people cannot find socially acceptable ways of feeding their egos, they sometimes turn to ways on which society frowns: to gang activities, and even to vice and crime. Above all, they seize on single, simple causes on which they can blame their frustrations. They look especially for persons or kinds of persons who can be used as scapegoats. These might be bosses, labor leaders, individual civic or political leaders, or they might be Catholics, Jews, Yankees, Britishers, or Negroes.

Scapegoats for ·Demagogs

As soon as people start thinking in terms of scapegoats, a demagog immediately appears who builds his power on this unmistakable indication of social sickness. Then comes the Adolf Hitler or Benito Mussolini, the Father Charles E. Coughlin, Rev. Gerald L. K. Smith, or Rev. J. Frank Norris, the Huey Long, Gerald Winrod, or Joe McWilliams.

But these developments may or may not lead to actual race riots. Such anti-racial feelings have been common enough in American history, as indicated by the "Know Nothings" of a century ago, the American Protective Association, the Ku Klux Klan, and the Black Legion; and all of these organizations were involved in religious and race riotings. But how does the riot pattern develop out of this "fascist atmosphere"? Why do people arrive at the point where they want to riot?

Nervous Tension

Riots are, as we said before, the end-products of thousands of little irritants in an atmosphere of growing tension. Riots are in the making when irritating frictions ignite latent intolerances between Negroes and whites. When the two races are not *consciously preparing themselves* to live democratically, frictions occur in overcrowded streetcars, parks, swimming pools, motion picture houses, restaurants, and the like. Riots are nearer when easy catchwords are used to sum up attitudes toward the other race and as explanations for irritating incidents. Negroes become "niggers." Whites become "pinks" and "ofays."* Because of lack of acquaintance on equal human terms with the members of the other race, myths of race differences become expletives and easy catch phrases. "Niggers are animals. They can't think. They don't know their place." "Whites are rotten and stiff-necked. They don't know that pink rule is on the skids."

Take such events and catch phrases, and then think of people with patience frayed by the fatigue of war-prolonged work-weeks and by the snapping of war-strained nerves and tempers. Think of the overcrowded dwellings for which exorbitant rent is paid and of competition to obtain such slum shelters. Think of the saloons, the pool parlors, and the movies as the only easily accessible recreational facilities to furnish much needed respite from these crowded living conditions. Think of being thrown into inter-racial job situations for the first time with no positive preparation for co-operation between Negroes and whites. Think of the tension that grips both races.

---

*While "ofay" is said by some to be "Pig Latin" for "foe," Walter White quotes James Weldon Johnson as observing that the term is a corruption of "au fait," French for "correct," and that Negroes used it satirically as a label for their white "superiors."

At such a time, a single spectacular event can unleash a torrent of accumulated emotional hatreds and bitternesses that can temporarily be directed—with little restraint—against an easy scapegoat.

This general pattern has flared on a number of occasions in Detroit in the past two years with increasingly bitter undertones. It has been the pattern in Los Angeles, certain cities in Texas, and elsewhere in the country. It is not just of local Detroit significance. Many of the irritants are common enough elsewhere and have been enjoying a lush growth throughout the country since the beginning of the war.

When President Franklin D. Roosevelt, on March 15, 1941, called for an end to "compromise with tyranny and the forces of repression," when he asked "every man and woman within our borders who loves liberty . . . to put aside all personal differences until victory is won," to have "no division of party, or section or race or nationality or religion," the Negro leaders talked about the American race record.

"Those are fine, thrilling words from Mr. Roosevelt," declared the April, 1941, *Crisis,* organ of the National Association for the Advancement of Colored People, but it added:

The trouble is that a great many people in this country have not understood what they mean. . . . On the very day Mr. Roosevelt spoke, Negro men were being denied employment in factories which are supposed to be intensely at work moving "products from the assembly lines of our factories to the battle lines of democracy." . . .

And all the while every avenue of communication is burdened with the sickening repetition that this "effort" is to defend and strengthen democracy.

Or as the editor of *Opportunity, Journal of Negro Life* (magazine of the National Urban League), put it at about the same time, "We have been aware . . . for a long time that a considerable section of America has already been conditioned to the Nazi conception of race." From long before the day that Crispus Attucks fell in the Boston Massacre, a Negro and the first martyr of the American Revolution, the Negro record of patriotism in this country has been convincing, but the Negroes wanted a chance to show it, not brush-offs.

Two years later, in the early months of 1943, opinion interviewers of a national polling agency discovered that 78 percent of the "sampled" Chicago and Detroit Negroes believed that they were not "getting as much chance as they should to help win the war." In three southern cities, the percentage was 53. Typical comments were:

"Colored folks is being ignored and mistreated."

"Because we are still segregated and not given the opportunity to really show how much we want to win the war."

"You gotta beg 'em to let us help fight, or do anything else to help win the war."

"And that's why it hurts when they take our boys."

These opinion interviewers added that the "satisfied few are either optimistic or self-critical" and gave these examples:

"Yes—we are getting the best chance we ever had."

"More and more we are getting opportunities."

"Yes—because if we have the qualifications, we'll do all right and get a chance. It's up to us to learn."

The percentage of dissatisfaction was much higher in Detroit (83%) than in Chicago (72%) in the spring of 1943, the opinion interviewers found.

Similar dissatisfactions existed elsewhere also, but the pot was boiling harder in Detroit, and it was there that it boiled over first. But the other pots—if we are not very careful—may follow the same course and continue to boil until some precipitating event sweeps the boiling brew over the edges. Then, after the break, a 16-year-old white boy may again be able to brag, as one did in Detroit:

I was rioting out there. Oh, there were about 200 of us in cars. We killed eight of 'em. I didn't kill any myself; I was too scared. I lost my nerve I guess, but my pals didn't.

I saw knives being stuck through their throats and heads being shot through, and a lot of stuff like that. It was really some riot.

They were turning cars over with niggers in them, you should have seen it. It was really some riot.

And rioters may again be able to gloat over their "victory." And as these mock-heroes swagger about, telling others of their mighty feats of prowess, they sow the seeds of another race conflagration—and the process is set in motion again.

So much for a brief glimpse of why people riot, of how rioting is stimulated by the conditions of war—even of a war for democracy. As an out-of-town newspaperman said of Detroit, and could have said of other war cities, it is "a tired place. It is full of frayed nerves from long hours and overwork. The people don't have anything to do after work. It's a war city."

That Detroit is a war city involves human factors that are far more significant than frayed work-weary nerves. Sociologists have pointed out* that our society actually lives in certain areas of its behavior according to two sets of patterns: the "spoken truths" or *overt morals* and the "unspoken truths" or *covert mores*. The former are what we hold forth as virtue policies in American life, and we mention them constantly when we refer to such things as equal economic opportunities for all, equal educational opportunities for all, pair-marriage, and the like. We speak of such things as features of our "way of life," and we take their existence for granted. We also, however, take for granted certain other principles that contradict some of these overt morals. For example, we know, as matters of fact, that equal economic opportunities and equal educational opportunities by no means exist for all Americans; that a very high percentage of American "pair-marriages" do not preserve that matrimonial ideal. And our individual and group behavior reflects these unspoken covert mores much more than it reflects the overt morals about which we are so glib and garrulous.

The effect of World War II on the status of the Negro constitutes a profound illustration of the operation of one of these deep and unspoken thought-patterns of American society. The war inevitably improved the financial lot of the Negro. Not only did his spiritual allegiance become necessary to the total war effort; his labor became an essential part of the manpower pool, and he is being rewarded more adequately than ever before in his experience.

This sudden gain in status, which violates one of the underlying prejudices of millions of Americans, evokes a powerful reaction. This reaction expresses itself in innumerable small and large actions on the part of sizable backward sections of the white population that resent the violation but find themselves unable to satisfy this resentment through socially acceptable acts. These white elements, therefore, are conditioned to react far more sensitively than before the change in the status of the Negro. Irritations multiply because these white elements are conditioned to be irritable upon the slightest provocation—or no provocation at all. The Negro, in turn, conscious of his improved situa-

---

* See the Waller-Lee distinctions between opinions and sentiments in Chapter 9, below. See also the Institute for Propaganda Analysis *Bulletin,* "American Common Sense," *Propaganda Analysis,* Vol. IV, No. 8 (June, 1941). The classical treatise on this general subject is W. G. Sumner's *Folkways* (Ginn & Company, 1906). *The Autobiography of Lincoln Steffens* (Harcourt, Brace, 1931) contains vivid illustrations of cultural duality, as does Robert S. Lynd's *Knowledge for What?* (Princeton University Press, 1939).

tion, no longer accepts discourtesies, incivilities, and bolder provoca-
tions from white elements without fairly aggressive protest or retalia-
tion. Having been graduated somewhat from previous servility or at
least having had his insecurity mitigated somewhat, the Negro is now
more inclined to "strike back." He is also more sensitive to the way
white people treat him. He is aware of his improved education and of
his increased political power. And the inevitable consequence is an
enormous multiplication in surface conflicts (as expressed in racial
frictions) as well as a deepening in the antagonism between backward
white elements and the Negroes with whom they come in contact.

When we understand these deeper currents in the bi-racial life in
a war city of 1943, we recognize that race riots are not isolated
phenomena. We realize that strife may be brewing in widely separated
areas of our country, owing to such subtle factors. We know that
America must learn from the tragic events of June 21st in Detroit.

And what are the results of such riots? What do people think they
will get out of them? What do they cost a community, the nation?
Let us see.

Chapter 2

WHAT DO RIOTS COST US?

TWO Negro boys, 11 and 12 years of age, will remember Detroit's Bloody Monday throughout their lives.

Their mother, Mrs. Ross Hackworth, was worrying about her sister who lived in the midst of the rioting area of June 21, 1943. Her husband finally consented to drive her over to see if her sister were safe.

All went well until after the Hackworths had started home. Then, as the Negro *Michigan Chronicle* described it, the husband "drove by a circuitous route to avoid the danger zones—or so he thought," but a "colored youth among the rioters, mistaking Mrs. Hackworth for white, hurled a brick into the car. . . . The missile struck her in the right temple, crushing her skull and severing an artery."

This exemplifies the blind brutality as well as the human costs of a race riot. It suggests the bitterness with which two boys, as they grow older, may think of the death of their mother.

It is, of course, all too easy to reduce the costs of a riot to statistics. It is much more difficult to see the human beings who are torn and twisted and warped. It takes imagination and insight to understand how such events as the Hackworth tragedy can drive members of the same community into two camps—with sympathy ever lessening between them. And it seems that we have to be shocked by vivid and tragic examples before we actually appreciate the impact upon war production—and what is most significant—upon soldier morale when the "people back home" start to shed each other's blood.

11

Absenteeism—Property Losses—Morale

Estimated absentee losses to the war effort during the first two days of Detroit's Race Riot Week came to at least one million man-hours. The Negro workers in particular were fearful of leaving their homes. Joseph D. Keenan, Vice-Chairman of the War Production Board, who announced this loss, put the total at what he called a figure greater than that of "all the labor disputes in the entire nation in the first two months of the year." And such losses to America do not include the costs of police, militia, Federal troops, courts, jails, hospital treatment, the destruction of stores, automobiles, and other property, and the wiping out of many other tangible and intangible values.

But far and above any property losses, however great, must be counted the cost of the Detroit riots and of all race riots in the destruction of human values. During a world war the disintegrative impact upon national morale is the chief of these human losses. In the case of Detroit, W. K. Kelsey of the Detroit *News*—respected as that paper's "Commentator"—on June 25th put it all very aptly:

There are thousands of whites who resent the claims of the Negro to social and even industrial equality. There are thousands of Negroes who resent the discrimination which makes it so hard for them to obtain, or having obtained, to keep employment among white workers, commensurate with their ability.

As one put it to the Commentator: "When such things happen as occurred Monday, many a Negro feels he'd just as soon fight and die as keep up the struggle peacefully." That is a terrible and desperate thought; but there it is. Should there be any reason or occasion for it, in a civilized community in the nation which considers itself the most enlightened in the world?

Or, as "A DETROIT SOLDIER" wrote to the Detroit *News* on July 6, from Auburn, Alabama, "Why can't people who live in one and the same country, which is supposed to be based on equality, get along?" He also mentioned his shame that his buddies could taunt him and his fellow Detroiters "that Detroit is a town where civilization still isn't advanced," and added, "What can we say?"

Weighing these human costs a little more systematically, we might say that they revolve around four interrelated sets of consequences of the riots. These can be labeled as follows:

1. *Individual insecurity*—especially as expressed in fear and distrust of Negroes by whites and whites by Negroes.

2. *Social paralysis*—a tightening of the automatic controls exercised

by society over its members, until these controls suppress any change whatever and all constructive social policies. These controls include gossip, censure, intolerance, and ostracism. They are popular and thus automatic rather than deliberate.

3. *Degradation of democracy as a symbol*—the loss of repute by the city in the eyes of the nation and of the nation in the eyes of a world that looks to it for democratic example and leadership.

4. *Dangers to democracy itself*—the intensification of irrational group loyalties, which manifest themselves in hatred and distrust of other groups. Gulfs between groups thus deepen, and dangers arise of inter-group conflicts on other than racial issues. Riots thus beckon demagogs to fertile soil for their divisive propaganda.

1. Individual Insecurity

In developing these conceptions a little further, we must recognize that the element of individual insecurity and its expression in fear and distrust of a member of another race were powerful elements in the propaganda armory of Hitler and Göbbels early in their campaign for German and then world domination. An immediate consequence of a race riot is that no white will walk or drive through a Negro area and that no Negro will leave the Negro area without conscious concern for his welfare. And this tension, distrust, and divisiveness erect high and stubborn barriers to the development of any democratic basis for mutual human understanding.

The barriers reared by this divisive insecurity permit a kind of paralysis to creep into the minds of men and to limit sharply their freedom of thought and action. Barriers make for ignorance, and ignorance invites blind feeling to dominate mental processes. *Hysterical individual insecurity thus leads to the kinds of emotional drives to which individuals and their leaders find they must give some expression—and then, more and more drastic expression.*

This element of individual insecurity and its related costs to human welfare and social health promote something that sociologists have called "social distance," an expressive term that stands for the barriers of fear and hate and ignorance which block people from knowing one another. The meaning of this term is heightened by the hypocrisy of such expressions as: "Some of my best friends are Jews." "Some of my most trusted employees are Negroes." "One of my oldest friends is Aunt Jessie." These expressions imply that Jews and Negroes in the bulk conform to the nasty stereotypes or catchwords of the Jew-baiters and Negro-beaters, and the same can be said of similar statements no doubt made by certain Negroes about occasional white people and by certain Jews about occasional Gentiles.

In short, the patterns of insecurity—always present to some extent —are enormously intensified by a riot. They leave consequences that fester deeply in the community, consequences that must be diagnosed and treated carefully so that they will not become permanent characteristics and so that they will not thus lead to even more vicious outbreaks.

2. Social Paralysis

The second social consequence of race riots may strike some as a strange one until they consider it. A tightening of the automatic controls exercised by society over its members may impress some people as being desirable. But is it a good idea? Such a tightening means more conformity to group and community ideas of what is right and wrong; it means higher penalties for pioneering ideas, regardless of their potential usefulness; and it means a cracking down on those who advocate courageous, far-seeing, or advantageous social policies. It means the placing of a premium on the tradition-minded, the die-hard, the dull cog, the petty authoritarian with his sadistic delight in exercising his power.

To illustrate, recall the way in which newspaper stories of "immoral youth"—whether the "flappers" of the 1920's or their sons and daughters, the jitterbugs and zoot-suiters of the 1940's—have made our elders try to tighten their controls over their progeny, their notions of "bringing back" the morality of the "good old days." Think of the way in which the waywardness of one son or daughter of a minority group in your home town reinforced existing prejudices and gave new grist to intolerant gossips; the culprit immediately injured his whole minority group, whether it be Negro or Irish, Baptist or Jewish or Catholic, Yankee or Italian. The petty authoritarians of our society relish new excuses for oppressing the youth and for ostracizing minorities.

Professor Zechariah Chafee, Jr., of the Harvard Law School, has told in his famous book on *Free Speech in the United States* of the tragic losses to American society produced by such authoritarianism. He shows how the penalizing by society of one brave humanitarian makes a thousand or a million more cautious men—men with families and responsibilities—bury even more deeply their ideas for social betterment, their small but useful contributions to a better and more healthful society.

What is more, not only the leader or exponent of social reform is afflicted with this excessive caution. As a result of the race riots, those governmental and societal agencies which are charged with the responsibility of implementing forward-looking social policy fear to continue their work even at the pace that had been socially acceptable before the riots. Any program of action therefore which is of benefit to one of the races has more of a tendency to arouse the intensified displeasure of extreme racists in the other group, with consequent threats of political reprisals against those agencies and their personnel. Thus, for a long time following race riots, the schools, housing authorities, departments of parks and recreation, health authorities, vocational and employment departments—all experience a freezing process during which they feel compelled to leave things at *status quo* or even to do nothing to improve conditions for one of the races and to bring about better understanding between the two. They are more than ever likely to say, "After all, the situation is just too hot right now."

Here again, in this group of consequences, are human and societal wounds that must be diagnosed and treated. If left alone, they would lead to the blocking of constructive change, an attempt at freezing the social order. They might even lead to a drive to turn the clock back, as in Fascist Italy and Nazi Germany.

3. Degradation of Democracy as a Symbol

The third group of consequences, those relating to a city's and nation's prestige, represents tragic losses which are the most difficult to restore. Such a melodramatic event as a race riot points all too vividly to the long-tolerated chasms between democratic words and undemocratic deeds, and it widens these chasms. Possibly more than at any other significant place in the nation, these discrepancies between hollow cry and fulsome act injure Army morale.

With the Kansas City *Star*, one realizes this fact with horror: "The enemy is . . . making propaganda use of these disorders, in Africa, Asia, and Latin-America." We must also face the manner in which northern enemies of constructive social change and southern beneficiaries from the "nigger-exploitation" and "share-cropper" systems can utilize such propaganda. An example of such a northern usage is the editorial statement in the Chicago *Tribune* which pointed to the Detroit riots as evidence of our inability to solve interracial problems in America and hence of the undesirability of attempting "an organic union with other countries whose peoples know nothing about our languages and institutions." As the *Tribune* put it, "The advocates of super-governments ask us to believe that what we have not yet accomplished in America can be achieved with the stroke of a pen on an international treaty." *Race riots thus become the basis for an attack upon any kind of international co-operation.* The southern "aristocrat's" use of the riots for propaganda purposes is a similar subversion; as the editor of the Atlanta *Constitution* rather sneeringly put it, "Detroit is learning what the South learned years ago." He presumably refers to the way of life that Ku Klux Klanism forced upon the Negro after his brief enfranchisement following the "War Between the States."

The third group of consequences, like the second, includes still more wounds to society—but far more universal ones—that must be diagnosed, treated, and cured. Even more. It includes blows to the beneficial influences of the United States in its world role, that can be offset only by counter-efforts, by positive events of an even more dramatic character, so as to restore America's reputation as the friend of the weak and the oppressed.

4. Dangers to Democracy Itself

Not only is democracy endangered as a symbol of the hopes of Americans and of those who believe in it and in Americans throughout the world; democracy itself, its very nature and substance, is placed in grave danger by race riots. An appeal, signed by Dr. William Allan Neilson and 137 other outstanding leaders of American life, makes this significance quite clear. Speaking of the Detroit race riots, the appeal tells how the "shock" of those riots "was all the greater because our country is now in the midst of a struggle of life and death with . . . dictatorships run on the 'master race' theory." The appeal adds that, unchecked, the threats implied in such riots may "bring down in ruin our Constitution, our Bill of Rights, and our Declaration of Independence, along with man's best hope for a government of freedom, dignity and security regardless of race, creed, or color."

This fourth group of consequences of race riots represents the really fundamental problem. The way to cure such wounds to society is to use every means at our disposal to make sure that democracy is given a better and better chance to function and thus to prove itself.

These are real challenges both to Detroit and to America. America must learn from Detroit. It is a grave national responsibility. We must really know and understand what happened in Detroit. We must lose no time in learning how to cope with the riot pattern wherever found. We must devise a technique for action—a preventive program. Toward such purposes this book is directed.

What do riots cost us? One brief chapter naturally cannot encompass the vast ramifications of that subject. We shall come to this subject again and again throughout this book, but before leaving this chapter let us look briefly at three facts that emerge sharply from this consideration of human and property wreckage.

Equally significant as all the bloodshed and agony and the more psychological losses are these three facts:

1. No Negroes and whites who lived close together as neighbors showed any tendency to fight each other. This was reported by *Life* magazine, by various newspapers, and by students in the department of sociology at Detroit's Wayne University.

2. Negro and white students attended classes at Wayne University, throughout the day and evening of Bloody Monday, with no indications whatsoever of conflict. The students had learned how to be neighborly in their casual associations in school.

3. Whites and blacks worked in the war plants of the Arsenal of Democracy on Bloody Monday side by side, and there were no disorders, according to a statement issued by Major General Henry S. Aurand, commander of the Federal troops that "occupied" Detroit. A great many of these industrial employees had learned how to work in the same plant together and how to grant each other reasonable rights as human beings. In this they had been aided by wise policies of management and labor. As U. S. Attorney General Francis Biddle stated in a letter to President Roosevelt on July 15, 1943, "It is extremely interesting that there was no disorder within [Detroit] plants, where colored and white men worked side by side, on account of efficient union discipline."

In other words, people who live near each other or go to school together or work together feel none of the alleged "natural animosity" which so many people claim exists between races—a "natural animosity" that scientists have disproved a thousand times.

Let us now try to answer the question, What really happened in Detroit? Once we have a reasonably thorough understanding of the essential factors at work in a race riot (Part II), we shall be in a position to arrive at a program of prevention (Part III).

II. WHAT REALLY HAPPENED IN DETROIT?

Chapter 3

DID THE RIOTS START
AT BELLE ISLE?
A CHRONOLOGY

"A CROWD of fifty whites were chasing a small colored boy. I started to try to help him and to find out about the trouble he was in, but whites and Negroes came up fast, and before I knew what was going on I'd been knocked down. They scratched my face and half tore my dress off of me. Then the fights started to spread all over the island."

Such was a Negro woman's recollections of her part in the events at Detroit's Belle Isle Park on the humid Sunday evening of June 20, 1943.

But the tribulations of the small colored boy and the Negro woman were not the only or the first sparks that flared into race riots that evening. There were many sparks, much smoldering intolerance and resentment. Four complaints of insult and injury had been lodged with the Belle Isle police by both Negroes and whites several hours before the rioting broke out.

Versions of the chief incident that precipitated riots on the bridge leading to Belle Isle, Detroit's 985-acre playground and beach, differ widely. Here are the versions gathered by one investigator:

Newspaper report: A fist fight between a Negro and a white man.
Frequent popular versions: A Negro baby thrown from the bridge by whites. A white baby thrown from the bridge by Negroes.
Other versions: Two white women attacked on bridge by Negroes. Sailors insulted white girls and Negroes got in between. White girls attacked by Negroes while swimming.

The entire account on page 1 of the Detroit *Free Press* the following morning of the first scenes in Detroit's Bloody Week is reproduced herewith. It gives the more generalized version that "several youths

Call 50 Police to Bridge Riot

More than 50 Detroit police were called to the Belle Isle Bridge a few minutes before midnight Sunday to quell a racial disturbance. Preliminary reports to the police indicated that several youths had been stabbed in a fight between Negroes and whites.

The fight later spread to Gabriel Richard Park near the Naval Armory and all precincts were asked to send reserves.

Free Press, June 21, 1943,
Final Edition

had been stabbed in a fight between Negroes and whites," according to preliminary police reports.

Wayne County Prosecutor William E. Dowling and Detroit Police Commissioner John H. Witherspoon pondered the matter for a month and then came to a conclusion that undoubtedly furnished deep moral satisfaction to the white rioters. According to the Detroit *Times* of July 17, the Prosecutor and Commissioner "agreed that Negroes were responsible for the recent race rioting in the city." As Dowling put it,

The Sunday night of the riot, a gang of colored boys and girls ranging from 13 to 20 years went to Belle Isle with the expressed purpose of driving the white people from the island. They started out, knowing that 85 per cent of the approximately 100,000 people on the island were colored, and beat up a white boy.

Next, they attacked a man and his wife who were eating a picnic lunch. They went on around to the bridge and one of the colored girls was pushed into a white girl who was accompanied by a sailor. A fight followed and it spread across the bridge.

One of the colored boys raced downtown to a club and had it announced over the public address system that a Negro woman and her baby had been thrown into the river.

Then it started. By 4 a.m., 400 stores owned by whites in the colored district had been wrecked, looted, pillaged and destroyed. A street car had been stopped and 50 white factory workers were taken out and beaten. It was 5 a.m. before the whites started to retaliate.

But are any of these "versions" and explanations correct? Do they

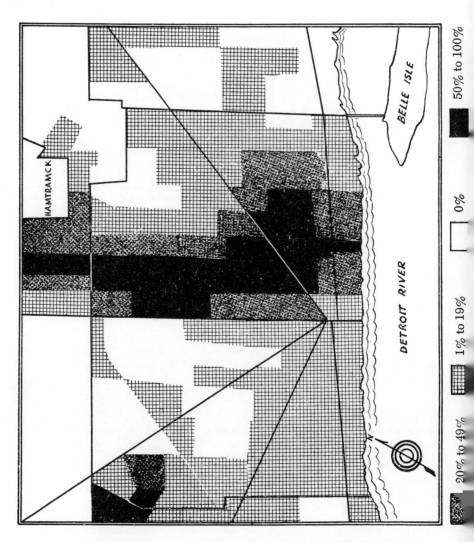

NEGRO RESIDENTIAL AREAS IN DOWNTOWN DETROIT

The chief area of Negro concentration surrounds and extends northwest from Paradise Valley. As the map on page 24 indicates, this is also Detroit's chief slum area. (Based on Detroit Real Property Survey, 1938)

This map represents 1938 conditions, but housing experts and social workers agree that the areas remain roughly the same and that the percentage of Negroes within the designated areas is higher today. (Prepared by the Real Property Survey and the Detroit Housing Commission.)

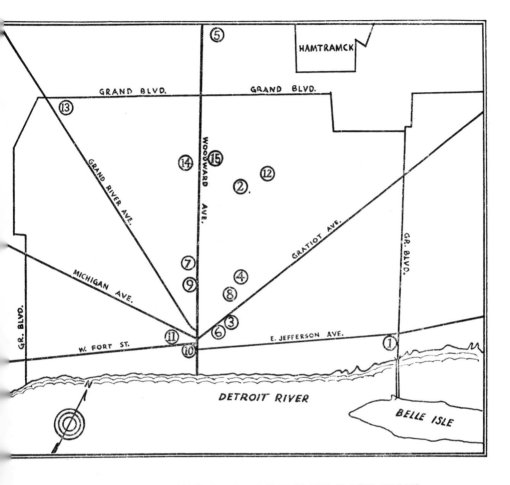

THE "BATTLE MAP" OF THE DETROIT RACE RIOTS

1. Belle Isle Bridge
   Jefferson and E. Grand Boulevard
   Naval Armory
2. Hastings and Forest
3. Receiving Hospital
4. Heart of Paradise Valley
5. Chevrolet Gear and Axle plant
6. Police Headquarters
7. Woodward-Davenport-Mack
8. St. Antoine (Negro) Y.M.C.A.
9. Woodward and Vernor
10. City Hall; Cadillac Square
11. Federal Building
12. Northeastern High School
13. Northwestern High School
14. Wayne University
15. Detroit Art Institute

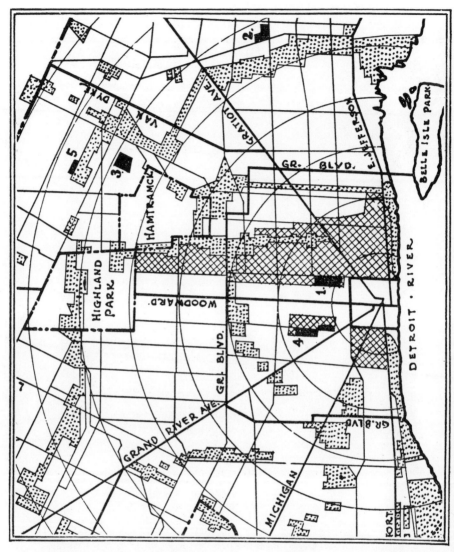

SLUM AND INDUSTRIAL
AREAS IN DOWNTOWN
DETROIT

Dotted: industrial areas
Cross-hatch: slum areas
Black: low-cost housing
     projects

1. Brewster and Douglas housing projects

2. Parkside projects

3. Charles project

4. Jeffries project

5. Sojourner Truth project

(Based on map of the Detroit
Housing Commission)

tell what really started the riots? Or did the race riots start long before, in events now only half remembered? Was the "emotional climate" of the riots prepared, as the Detroit *News* feature writer A. M. Smith contends, by the fighting words of the orators of the National Association for the Advancement of Colored People during its convention in Detroit's Olympia arena several weeks before? And what about the intolerant utterances over a period of years by Father Charles E. Coughlin of nearby Royal Oak, fomenter of the "Christian Front"? And what about those two inflammatory Protestant demagogs of Detroit, the Reverends Gerald L. K. Smith and J. Frank Norris?

Or did the riots start as a result of smoulderings from previous racial clashes—such as the strike in the spring of 1941 in the Ford River Rouge Plant, where Negroes and whites were pitted against each other? Perhaps the trouble started in the race riot at Northwestern High School in 1941 and was fanned by the Mayor's failure to act on the findings of his investigating committee in that affair. Perhaps the enmity had been latent since the Sojourner Truth Housing riots early in 1942.

To judge from available facts, the race riots started at Belle Isle Bridge *only in a very specific sense:* in the sense that already-smouldering embers were suddenly fanned into bright flames and that hot winds scattered sparks throughout districts littered with the tinder of intolerance and bigotry. It could have been precipitated just as easily by any one of a dozen other incidents that occurred in Detroit during the preceding two years.

Detroit's race tensions had snapped from time to time even before the day in 1925 when a white mob tried to eject a Negro physician—Dr. Ossian Sweet—from a house he had bought in a white district. Reports on facts and preventive measures had been made from time to time, beginning with the "Report of the Mayor's Committee on Race Relations: *Embodying findings and recommendations based upon a survey of race conditions in the city, undertaken in 1926,*" published March 10, 1927, but dealing with the 1925 Sweet incident. And such reports not only took a long time to prepare; for practical purposes, they were ignored.

But let us reconstruct as accurate a chronology as possible of the events of Sunday evening, June 20, 1943, and of the days that followed, days of race rioting, of buck-passing, of brave deeds, of "noble" statements to cover ineffectualities, of searches for a scapegoat, and of the whitewashing of gangster tactics by those who were paid to support law and order for all the citizens. Let us piece the story together, scene by scene, to the extent necessary to give an over-all perspective, and then let us attempt to analyze such facts and to find answers to these questions: How were the riots handled? Who did the rioting? Who were the casualties? What did the riots do to Detroit? What really caused the riots?

SUNDAY, JUNE 20, 1943

10:30 P.M. "When the first police arrived on the [Belle Isle] bridge," Senior Police Inspector Jesse Meade said, "approximately 200 sailors were fighting with Negroes, and white men and Negroes were rushing into the fight." The rioting then gradually spread into adjacent Gabriel Richard Park, between the mainland side of the bridge and the Naval Armory, and all police precincts were asked to send reserves. Five thousand persons were involved, and some thirteen whites and blacks were known to have received lacerations and contusions.

10:45 P.M. A Negro co-ed of Wayne University, Detroit's large municipal school, told the following eye-witness story of the Belle Isle riot's early stages:

At about 10:45 on Sunday night we left the island and drove over the bridge towards home. At Jefferson Avenue [near the bridge] a considerable crowd had gathered, and the line of cars moved very slowly.

I saw a colored fellow standing in the crowd and called out to him asking what the matter was. He yelled back, "Nothing," and waved us on. It looked like a fight between Negroes and whites that would make a story for the Negro paper my father publishes; so after we'd gotten by the intersection, we drove up a block and started to circle around in order to get another look at the thing. But at the first corner we saw a gang of white youths beating up a young Negro, and there were cries of "Kill the black bastard!"

The white toughs looked almost insane. So we quickly drove home, and I immediately began to call up my friends to tell them to stay in their homes because real trouble was brewing. We've really had trouble ever since that Naval Armory was erected there.

11 P.M. Miss Gladys House and a crippled male friend, both Negroes, went to Belle Isle at 7 p.m., "canoed quite some time and started . . . home at 11 p.m." In a sworn affidavit, Miss House later recalled her experiences in the Bridge Battle as follows:

As we walked across the bridge I noticed several white adults chasing a small colored boy, who appeared to be about 12 years of age. At this time I didn't realize what was going on, so I stepped aside to allow the crowd to pass us. We then continued to walk across the bridge when suddenly the mob realized that we were colored also and began to approach us saying, "We don't want any niggers on Belle Isle."About this time they began to attack us. The mob told us to run, but we were unable to because my escort is a victim of osteomyelitis since a mere child, making it necessary for him to wear a special made shoe. At this time several white girls began to beat me on my head with their fists while the white mob of boys jumped on my escort and began kicking and beating him in his face until he had fallen to the ground.

I noticed a policeman on the bridge, directing traffic; I called to him for aid. He nonchalantly came to our assistance and placed us in a scout car and drove us to Jefferson Avenue, at which place he told us we could catch a street car to go home. It was at this time that I noticed my head was bleeding so I asked the officer to take us to the Receiving Hospital. The officer began to give several excuses as to why he would be unable to take us to the hospital. I found that it was necessary for me to insist, by telling him that I wasn't going to get out of his car until he carried us to the hospital. The officer then transferred us to another scout car, which car took us to the hospital.

During the time of the attack on us, I happened to notice that there were several hundred white people standing at the entrance of the bridge waiting to attack Negroes as they came along. In the meantime, there were several scout cars at the entrance of the bridge, not allowing any persons to cross the bridge to the island; but were doing nothing to disperse the crowd on the bridge.

11:30 P.M. Small fighting units east and west of the Belle Isle Bridge on Jefferson Avenue were broken up by the city police, but from a dozen other sections of the city reports of rioting were telephoned to Police Headquarters, and scout cars were dispatched to intercept rumored carloads of Negroes armed with clubs and pipes. Also, at about this time, one Leo Tipton, a Negro, is said to have grabbed a microphone in a Negro night club and urged the 500 patrons "to take care of a bunch of whites who killed a colored woman and her baby at Belle Isle Park. (County Prosecutor Dowling had Tipton arrested for this act, on July 30.) The rumor Tipton thus circulated was as false as its white counterpart disseminated at about the same time: that Negroes had raped and killed a white woman on the bridge.

SUMMARY: *In an hour and a half, a fight at Belle Isle Bridge had spread north, east, and west, especially into the Negro ghetto. A rumor had been planted in the minds of 500 Negroes in Paradise Valley and had shocked them into action. Another rumor had circulated rapidly among whites as they left plants before midnight in the "Arsenal of Democracy." The dynamite had exploded. Hysterical people had car-*

ried the flames into the focal points of intolerance, economic and social insecurity—the degrading congestion of the slums.

MONDAY, JUNE 21, 1943: EARLY MORNING

12:30 A.M.   Overtaxed city police were dispatched to intersections along Hastings and St. Antoine Streets, in the congested Negro (urban) area called Paradise Valley. Three police cars were sent to the intersection of Forest and Hastings Streets on a report that a crowd of 500 Negroes had assembled there. The story that three Negroes had been killed at Belle Isle spread rapidly in this crowd. . . . As factory workers drove along the city's main midtown east-west traffic arteries—Forest and Warren Avenues and Vernor Highway—Negroes began to stone white cars.

1 ' A.M.   Negro rioters roamed north and south along Hastings Street. They stabbed a white man in the chest. A policeman suffered a possible skull fracture. Injured people were being taken to Detroit's municipal Receiving Hospital at the rate of *one a minute.* But in the densely populated and racially mixed area in the western part of the city, life went on in a normal and peaceful fashion: Those people slept.

2 A.M.   Negroes stopped an eastside streetcar and stoned white factory workers inside. Employees coming from work at the Chevrolet Gear and Axle Plant on Holbrook, *three miles north of the heart of Paradise Valley,* were attacked by a Negro mob.

3 A.M.   Large groups of Negroes began to loot stores and destroy white property on Hastings Street. Inspector Fred Stephan reported to Police Commissioner Witherspoon that *the situation was out of control,* especially in Paradise Valley. As one white Detroit leader pointed out, the Negroes were "turned back into their own residential districts" and then "began taking their spite and resentment out on 'white' stores and properties," especially on stores "of a decidedly exploitative character."

4 A.M.   At Woodward and Charlotte Avenues white mobs began to stone the automobiles of passing Negroes. Negroes attending the all-night Roxy and Colonial theaters on Woodward Avenue were systematically beaten as they emerged onto the sidewalk.

At about this time, Police Commissioner Witherspoon said that there appeared "evidence of retaliatory action by whites." . . .

I couldn't sleep [recalled a white Wayne University graduate student later] so about three o'clock I drove down to Harper Hospital where my wife was confined after the birth of our child. I went up to her ward, talked to the nurse, found out everything was all right, and left for a cup of coffee on Woodward Avenue. I was on my way to Greenfield's—right next to the Roxy. A big gang of white people was in front of the theater, and every time a Negro came out into the light they ganged up on him.

"There were three scout cars there, two in front of the show and one across the street. After I'd seen several of these beatings—and they'd hit the guy until he dropped—I went up to a scout car and suggested that they escort the Negroes out of the show all at one time—sort of give them "safe conduct" in a body to the other side of Woodward. The policeman in the car only shrugged his shoulders and said, "See the Chief about it!"

When the Governor's Fact-Finding Committee finally issued its report on August 11 and gave the official version of these Woodward incidents, its statement was briefly as follows:

When . . . whites were observed assaulting colored patrons leaving the Roxy and Colonial Theatres on Woodward Avenue, in addition to arresting white persons, the police entered the theatres and instructed the colored folk to remain there until adequate police protection could be assured them on leaving. Police officers were stationed at the exits to insure protection.

Police Commissioner Witherspoon held a meeting of law enforcement officials at this time (4 a.m.) in his office at Police Headquarters. Mayor Edward J. Jeffries; Colonel A. M. Krech, U. S. Army commander of the Detroit area; John Bugas, special agent in charge of the local office of the Federal Bureau of Investigation; Captain Donald Leonard of the Michigan State Police; and Wayne County Sheriff Andrew C. Baird attended. These men discussed in detail how and under what circumstances Federal troops might be brought in. Colonel Krech assured the Mayor that the military police battalions stationed at Rouge Park could be on patrol duty in Detroit 49 minutes after a request had cleared from the Mayor through the Governor to the proper U. S. Army officials. *But they did not try out this procedure at this time.*

6:15 A.M. A Negro died at Edith K. Thomas Hospital from loss of blood. He was said to have cut his leg on the broken glass of a store window.

6:30 A.M. The conference in Commissioner Witherspoon's office ended. The Commissioner decided that a let-up had occurred in the "serious rioting." Despite the statement by his Inspector at 3 a.m.— only three hours earlier—that the situation was out of control, he now thought that the "situation was under control. Later the rioting increased. . . . A sergeant and a patrolman in the department were shot . . . trying to disperse a mob of Negroes at Hastings and Division; the assailant was killed." And still the Federal troops were not called!

SUMMARY: *Negroes had begun to stone white cars and to destroy white-owned property in Paradise Valley. By 3 a.m., the Police Commissioner regarded the situation as out of control. An hour later, whites had begun to gang up on isolated Negroes along Woodward Avenue. The Commissioner called a meeting in his office and decided not to ask for Federal troops because he now thought the situation was under control.*

MONDAY, JUNE 21, 1943: MORNING

8:30 A.M. "A Negro delegation," stated an informant, "went to see the Mayor and asked him to call troops to quell the rioting. The Mayor seemed reluctant to do this." But the Mayor did accept an invitation from the group to attend a meeting of the Detroit Citizens' Committee (a bi-racial body) at noontime.

Rev. Horace White, pastor of Plymouth Congregational Church and an active leader among the Negroes, toured the Paradise Valley district in a sound car, exhorting his fellow Negroes to calm themselves, to have faith in the decent majority among their white neighbors and fellow-townsmen. The Detroit Citizens' Committee also had quantities of handbills printed and distributed in the same area.

9 A.M. At the Police Commissioner's request, Mayor Jeffries telephoned Governor Harry F. Kelly, who was attending the Conference of Governors at Columbus, Ohio, and asked that Federal troops be summoned. The Governor transmitted this plea by telephone to the Sixth Service Command Headquarters at Chicago. He also ordered Michigan State Troops and Police to Detroit. "Police Commissioner Witherspoon and I knew at 9 a.m.," Mayor Jeffries said, "that we needed more man power and that we needed it quickly. We saw that mechanically the Police Department was unable to cope with the problem."

10 A.M. George Stark, Detroit *News* staff writer, was injured in the following manner, to quote his paper:

Stark said a Negro was driving a car just ahead of him and slowed down "almost to a walk," when another Negro threw a stone at him from the sidewalk. The stone struck Stark over the right eye. A moment later, he was struck near the base of the skull by another stone.

"A gang of Negroes suddenly seemed to assemble from nowhere at all," he said. "They dragged me from the car and were roughing me up when three policemen appeared and rescued me."

11 A.M. When the Governor arrived by plane from Columbus, Colonel Krech was holding a conference in his downtown office which Kelly joined. Federal troops, he learned, could not be deployed into an area *unless martial law was first declared. Governor Kelly was reluctant to suspend state and local laws.* On this situation "Commentator" W. K. Kelsey of the Detroit *News* later observed in a personal statement, by way of clarification:

[Mayor Jeffries] disagreed with Gov. Kelly on Monday, Kelly insisting that there be no imposition of martial law, Jeffries arguing that it was necessary to obtain reinforcements as soon as possible, regardless of the steps required. Kelly insisted that State Troops would soon control the situation. Jeffries was doubtful. Kelly was the only official who could ask for Federal help.

Gangs of white hoodlums were stopping and burning Negro cars on Woodward Avenue, the city's main north-south thoroughfare. Young white toughs began preying on isolated Negro males who, ignorant of the riot situation, had ventured into the downtown area. Tear gas dispersed several such aggregations.

Judges assembled in the Police Commissioner's office for a conference and witnessed from there a small riot at Brush Street and Gratiot Avenue: whites attacking a group of Negroes. Looking out of the Commissioner's office, they watched police break up the fight, arrest a half-dozen white men, and take them to headquarters.

SUMMARY: *Negroes had requested the Mayor to call Federal troops, but he had thought this would not be necessary. A Negro pastor toured Paradise Valley in a sound car, pleading for calmness. Governor Kelly requested Federal troops, but found he could not get them without declaring martial law. He refused to make such a declaration. White hoodlums in gangs were burning Negro cars and preying on isolated Negro males.*

MONDAY, JUNE 21, 1943: NOON

12 M., NOON. Mayor Jeffries attended an emergency meeting of the Detroit Citizens' Committee, an inter-racial body formed at the time of the Sojourner Truth Housing race riots early in 1942. The group had assembled at the Lucy Thurman (Negro) branch of the Y.W.C.A. in order to bring some order into the chaotic conditions at-

tending the rioting. Jeffries arrived at the building escorted by three police scout cars.

At this meeting, R. J. Thomas, President of the United Automobile Workers' Union (C.I.O.) made a strong speech, liberally sprinkled with "cuss words," in which he demanded a stoppage of the bloodshed. Albert Pelham, a prominent Negro, tried to get the Negro leaders present to ask for martial law, but he was opposed by the Rev. Horace White, Negro pastor, who claimed that the police and Negro auxiliaries could do the job. As White later stated,

> My stand was that we should not have out-right martial law which would slow up production, would curtail business, stop the courts, and make things be a long time coming back to normal. I felt it unwise to declare out-right martial law in this defense area, without other means being tried to secure order. In addition to this, martial law has always worked to the detriment of the Negro people. I know that southern soldiers seek to give vent to their feelings about Negroes during such a period. . . .

Thomas mobilized opposition in the U.A.W.-C.I.O. to the race riots through calling an emergency meeting of the union's shop stewards. Later the U.A.W.-C.I.O. further implemented its efforts by issuing "a call for a conference of all U.A.W. educational directors and chairmen in Wayne County. Purpose: to determine immediate steps for intensifying the union's educational program for building labor unity between men and women of all races on the basis of their common interests as workers who must stand together regardless of provocation."

The noon edition of the Detroit *Times* carried a story under a two-column head that asserted Negroes had murdered a police sergeant. Actually the police sergeant, although desperately wounded, was still alive. . . .

According to one of the authors of this book (N. D. Humphrey),

> There was an automobile burning on Woodward and up a side street a Negro was being horribly beaten. Eventually the mob let the Negro go, and he staggered down to the car tracks, and he tried to get on a streetcar. But the car wouldn't stop for him.
>
> The Negro was punch-drunk. There were policemen down the street, but they didn't pay any attention to him.
>
> I started shouting, "Hey, copper. Hey, copper." And I pointed to the Negro in the middle of the street. The policeman finally took notice of me, but instead of going in the direction in which I was pointing he walked over to his parked scout car. Then two huge hoodlums began to slug the Negro, and he hung there on the side of the safety zone, taking the punches

as if he were a bag of sand. That infuriated me, and I yelled even louder to the cops, all the time gesturing towards the Negro.

Finally the police started walking slowly toward the fight, which in the meantime had moved down the street. Then the crowd started pushing me around, but I kept moving and kept my fists up near my chest, and the crowd moved after the much tastier and more permissible Negro game.

The crowds of whites were increasing in size on Woodward Avenue. Milling packs of human animals hunted and killed any of the easily visible black prey which chanced into the territory. Whether formally affiliated or not, the hoodlums operated in gangs *under informal but definite leadership*. As one white Southerner bragged to a barber, his eyes shining with fanatical excitement, "Why the gang I was in on Woodward Avenue must have killed at least twenty-five of them." Little wonder that rumors of hundreds of people slaughtered spread widely.

SUMMARY: *An inter-racial committee met with the Mayor in the Negro Y.W.C.A. R. J. Thomas demanded decisive action. A Negro pastor requested Negro auxiliaries to aid the City Police. A local paper prematurely announced the death of a police sergeant. The major part of the police force was concentrated in the eastside area, but the looting there of white stores by blacks continued. White crowds were increasing on Woodward Avenue. White hoodlums hunted and beat down any of the easily visible black prey they chanced to see.*

MONDAY, JUNE 21, 1943: AFTERNOON

1 P.M. "That nigger Preacher [Horace] White has had it too much his own way in this town," bragged a swaggering white real estate operator, originally from Texas, "but I fixed it for him and the Mayor Monday afternoon. Know what I did? I got a bunch of the boys from the automobile factories to go out and call the Mayor's office on pay 'phones: They'd say, 'Is this the Mayor's office?' And then they'd say, 'Well, let me speak to Mayor White.' When the secretary'd get confused over that, they'd say, 'Well, if he's not there, let me have his assistant, Mr. Jeffries.' I tell you, that preacher and those Jews up along Joy Road are ruining the niggers and the town with them." White is a prominent Detroit Negro minister and civic leader.

A white university student "saw colored men on Hastings dart back and forth across the street, going from doorway to doorway. There was a furniture store across the street with a small hole in the window in the morning. As people walked by, they each made the hole a little bigger, until by 4 o'clock the hole was big enough for the people to steal things out of the window. . . . At one time, I saw one colored boy running down Hastings with two large chunks of meat under his arms."

2 P.M. Sporadic looting of white stores continued in the eastside Negro area. No Negro stores were touched. The stores were easily available symbols of white dominance upon which to release pent-up hostilities. The word "Colored" had appeared earlier, painted on windows, often in the same fresh paint. "From a tavern on Hastings near Livingstone," a Negro newspaper reporter "saw men with arms full of liquor bottles run from the building while, just a few doors below, two men carried a quarter of beef through the smashed open front of what, until Sunday night, had been a grocery store." In other words, crudely organized gangs of Negro hoodlums began to operate more openly. Some looters destroyed property as if they had gone berserk.

Because of overcrowding, the high schools had been forced to dismiss many of their students for the day at 1:30 p.m., and they did so this day. Some of these youths joined 16-year-olds who had dropped out of school upon passing the compulsory attendance age, and thousands of adolescent white adventurers swarmed into the downtown area or ranged themselves along Woodward Avenue in search of excitement. Other lads—whites in black areas and blacks among whites—found themselves immediately on the defensive, as the following eye-witness account of a white school teacher indicates:

Jim was no more than out of the school yard when a white boy hit him in the stomach with a baseball bat. The Negro turned around and ran quickly to a parked car in which two women teachers were sitting. The teachers quickly let him into their car, but the driver in her excitement "flooded" the engine.

Meanwhile white rioters began to crowd around the car, and one who had an axe started to chop in the roof.

Before the mob got too large to "make a break through," the colored boy dashed for the school building. He entered it and locked the door. By this time a considerable gang had gathered on the front steps of the building, and the police were called to disperse the mob and take the boy to safety.

Two scout cars finally appeared, but none of the policemen did anything. The principal, impatient with the police, called out to them to escort the boy to safety. After much hesitation, a policeman yelled, "Take him around to the back, then, and we'll get him."

At the back door the officer yelled gruffly, "O.K., jerk, come here!"

The colored boy, obviously fearful of an antagonistic reception once he reached the scout car, held back. The principal thereupon gave the policeman a heated lecture on civility. When she was through the policeman asked the boy nicely to get into the car and promised to take him home safely.

At Briggs Stadium, home field for the Detroit Tigers, colored and white high school boys watched excitedly while Chadsey High was beating Pershing 6 to 3 for the Metropolitan League baseball championship. School loyalties were in friendly rivalry here, not race ties.

3 P.M. A colored co-ed "was riding south on a Beaubien streetcar. At one stop I was horrified to witness a group of my fellow Negroes stop a white driver, pull him from his automobile, and kick and beat him until he fell unconscious to the ground."

A white co-ed saw this:

The young Negro was being chased down the street by a gang of young whites who were brandishing knives. He was grey with fear. Saliva drooled from his mouth. His shirt had been half torn from him. The white pursuers were raving mad, with hatred blazing from their eyes. I didn't—or couldn't —continue to watch the thing. The whites probably caught him. They were gaining on him when I last looked, and there was nothing to stop them.

Many Negro leaders saw from the first the need for special Negro police to allay the fears of their fellows in Paradise Valley and to halt looting and hysterical shootings and mob clashes. Rev. Horace White had therefore earlier asked the Mayor and the Police Commissioner to deputize 250 Negro ministers and other responsible citizens to act as auxiliary policemen. Because such deputizing was not in line with law and precedent, the Commissioner offered as an alternative that 250 be given O.C.D. (Office of Civilian Defense) hats, and that some of them be also issued O.C.D. arm bands, but that all be made to understand that their duties and rights did not extend beyond peaceful patrolling and moral suasion. *They could not function as policemen.* At about 3 p.m., a rumor spread that a Negro mob was converging on Police Headquarters, at the southern end of Paradise Valley. Police went forth to meet the menace, only to learn that Pastor White was bringing down volunteers to serve as symbols of decent Negro leadership. Hats were passed around, and the Police Commissioner found a basis on which he issued night sticks and arm bands to 11 of Mr. White's chief associates.

4 P.M. Major General Henry S. Aurand had arrived by plane from Chicago to represent U. S. Army interests. Together with Governor Kelly and Mayor Jeffries, he discussed the problems that would be in-

volved in using Federal troops without declaring "full martial law."
Meanwhile 10,000 people jammed around the Woodward and Daven-
port-Mack intersection on the northern edge of the downtown district.
Cadillac Square—between City Hall and County Building—was packed
with milling murderous thousands, especially at the City Hall end.
Vicious anti-Jewish pamphlets were being passed among the rioters.

Some 800 Michigan State Troops were said by Lt. Gov. Eugene C.
Keyes to be assembled and placed on alert at the Piquette Armory.
This report was incorrect.

A group of churchmen, labor leaders, and representatives of youth
organizations met at St. John's Protestant Episcopal Church (Woodward at Vernor), and passed a resolution urging the Mayor to request
the Governor to proclaim martial law so that Federal troops might be
used, to broadcast an appeal for all persons to remain off the streets,
and to urge newspapers to refrain from inflammatory statements and
headlines. . . .

"The pastor of my church could pass for white," a Negro co-ed
stated. "Thank God, at least once in his life he did! He was on a
Woodward streetcar that awful Monday. A mob of crazy white men
boarded the car and asked if there were any 'niggers' on board. They
passed right by our pastor as they rushed through the car and didn't
even realize that he was colored." . . .

From the twentieth floor of a downtown office building one of the
authors of this book (A. M. Lee) watched the movements of mobs on
Washington Boulevard. He felt that he might have been observing
race riots taking place "on a laboratory table."

Without being able to understand the cries, it was obvious that one in
the mob would yell something like, "There's black meat! Let's get 'im!"
Then the hoodlums would spill like quicksilver toward that unfortunate.
The rioters, who immediately surrounded the victim, acted as though they
were embarrassed and didn't know what to do in most cases. Hoodlums
standing back in the gang would sidle toward the Negro and hit him from
behind an unwilling shield.

Then the police would come with tear gas and that particular demon-
stration would dissolve. But in a few moments you could see a leader running toward another Negro and gesticulating, and the quicksilver would
begin to pour towards that new focus. One had an overpowering sense of
irresponsibility, of Hallowe'en-marauding at its worst. It was hard to keep
from permitting the laboratory-table analogy to "get you," to convince your-
self that somehow those were human beings and not small laboratory animals
strangely different from guinea pigs.

5 P.M.   Radio bulletins announced that Mayor Edward J. Jeffries would broadcast an appeal to the city at 6:30 p.m. . . .

A white minister and his son "developed a system for rescuing imperiled Negroes. The clergyman—he is a well-known Protestant leader—would alight from his car, rush into the midst of white rioters and start arguing with them, quoting Scripture, and sermonizing for dear life." In the meantime, as he said, "while I talked to the crowd, my son would . . . pick up the colored man from the roadway and lead him into our car. Then we would drive off to a hospital." . . .

Negroes were not even safe near City Hall, fountainhead of law and order. One of the authors saw Negroes mauled and ineffectively protected by police at about this time near City Hall and again at about 7 p.m. . . .

W. K. Kelsey, "The Commentator" of the Detroit *News*, "happened to be in the City Hall Monday when a Negro started to leave the building. A white man stopped him.

" 'You'd better stay here awhile. I don't like the looks of that crowd on the corner. You'd be taking a chance.' The Negro thanked him and stayed."

By this time, sixteen automobiles driven by Negroes had been over-turned and burned on Woodward Avenue. . . . The fighting and the looting of white-owned stores in Negro neighborhoods continued. . . .

A white factory worker "saw one policeman march an injured Negro to a scout car and then, when the crowd closed in, turn the Negro back to the enraged mob." . . .

Large groups of whites on Woodward Avenue were beginning to form and march eastward toward John R. Street, and gangs of Negroes on Brush awaited the attack.

6:30 P.M.   Four white youths, aged 16 to 20 years, without provocation, shot down one Moses Kiska, a 58-year-old Negro, "just for the Hell of it." Kiska was merely waiting for a streetcar at Mack Avenue and Chene Street. As John McManis wrote in the Detroit *News* a month later, "Sociologists may be able to give it a name, but the layman never will understand how four ordinary boys could go out and . . . shoot down innocent people." One of the boys told their story thus:

We didn't have anything to do. We were just bumming around. Bob . . . and Blackie . . . were in the pool room. We wanted to see the fighting but we didn't want to go where we would get hurt.

We had my gun along. It was my car. Aldo was driving. Someone—
I don't know who—said: "Let's go out and kill us a nigger." We agreed that
it was a good idea.

We drove around for a long time. We saw a lot of colored people, but
they were in bunches. We didn't want any of that. We wanted some guy
all by himself. We saw one on Mack Avenue.

Aldo drove past him and then said, "Gimme that gun." I handed it over
to him and he turned around and came back. We were about 15 feet from
the man when Aldo pulled up, almost stopped and shot. The man fell and
we blew.

We didn't know him. He wasn't bothering us. But other people were
fighting and killing and we felt like it, too.

Harold True, radio newscaster, announced that State Police had
been warned to watch out for carloads of armed Negroes heading
for Detroit from Chicago. No source for his information was offered.
When a colleague of the authors telephoned True, immediately following the broadcast, the newscaster claimed that public interest
justified his announcement, its inflammatory effect notwithstanding.
True's report turned out to be inaccurate.

Mayor Jeffries followed True on the air with an appeal for a
return to sanity. He pointed out that the only ones who would benefit
from the strife were the Nazis and Japs. Over the same radio, Governor
Kelly issued a proclamation of "modified martial law." The Governor's
proclamation declared "A state of emergency and the necessity for the
armed forces of the State of Michigan to aid and assist, but in subordi-
nation thereto, all duly constituted civil authorities in the execution of
the laws of this State." He said that the "necessity for such aid" extended to the counties of Wayne (of which Detroit is the seat), Oakland, and Macomb.

The Governor also (1) banned the sale of alcoholic beverages
"until further notice"; (2) closed all amusement places "tonight at
9 o'clock" and ordered that they "remain closed until further notice";
(3) asked people "not having important business or going to or coming
from work" to stay at home from 10 o'clock that night until 6 the next
morning; and ordered such other necessary precautions as the prohibi-
tion on the carrying of "arms or weapons of any description" by others
than the police and military. But the Governor had not complied yet
with the prerequisites for bringing in Federal troops.

SUMMARY: *Lootings of white-owned stores and beatings of whites
continued throughout the Negro areas, with the whites on Woodward
Avenue and in the downtown district running more and more "hog*

wild." Some high school students, dismissed early as usual because *of the overcrowding of the school buildings, joined with 'teen-age out- of-school hoodlums to furnish recruits for the anti-Negro "crusade." A mile away from City Hall other Negro and white youngsters peace- fully watched high school baseball teams battle for the city champion- ship. Jittery whites almost mistook would-be volunteer Negro police auxiliaries as a gang of armed attackers. Ten thousand whites jammed the City Hall area, pulling Negroes off buses and streetcars. Civic leaders met and passed a resolution. A radio newscaster warned of an armed Negro invasion speeding from Chicago. The Governor pro- claimed "modified martial law."*

MONDAY, JUNE 21, 1943: EVENING

7:30 P.M. "Jeffries made an inspection trip up Woodward Ave- nue," to quote an account in the Detroit *News.* "Within five or six blocks north of Vernor highway, he saw seven automobiles overturned in the streets, many of them burned; an estimated crowd of 5,000 rioters, mostly [*sic*] white, in the streets; men stopping street cars by pulling trolleys off the wires, and removing and beating Negro pas- sengers; gangs pursuing Negroes from Woodward Avenue toward John R. and Brush Streets." . . .

A Negro girl who was hidden in the attic of the Roxy Theater by its manager, told this story of the same rioting:

> From where I was hidden . . . I could see white people beating up any Negro caught on the street. They caught one old couple coming out of a store and beat the man until he was unconscious. . . . They ordered the woman to run and when she got a few yards, they caught up with her, pulled her hair and choked her until she slumped to the sidewalk. . . . Police were making no attempt to break up the crowd; they just milled around with the rioters.

8 P.M. "I called for Michigan State Troops who had been ordered mobilized at 10 a.m. by the Governor," Mayor Jeffries recalled in a "white paper" he issued more than a week later. "There were only 32 men [and not 800] available for duty at the Piquette Armory, and they were not mobile. . . .

"We needed desperately more manpower," he added. "The great mob on Woodward avenue was practically out of control. Our police force was behind barricades on Brush Street to keep the white mobs from invading colored residential areas." . . .

As Louis Martin, Editor of the Negro *Michigan Chronicle,* put it, "This mob of whites moved down from Woodward and Eliot to Adelaide and John R. Police had thrown a cordon across Adelaide and tried to . . . persuade them to disperse. Instead, they turned . . . to a house and set it afire. . . . Earlier . . . a mob had swarmed through Eliot street, forcing me to leave the office . . . by the back door, leap over the back fence and make my escape through the alley. Two policemen were a few steps in front of the mob, with pistols drawn."

In the midst of all this violence, Raymond O. Hatcher, Group Work Secretary, Detroit Urban League, found events that the *Free Press* hailed as evidence of the "core of goodwill and understanding in Detroit." He found, for example, that a "group of Negro and white men, all members of Franklin Settlement House, [met Monday evening and] formulated . . . an appeal for democracy, reason and co-operation on the home front 'to protect our boys who are now giving their lives for this cause.'" This Neighborhood Committee on Race Relations circulated throughout an eight-block area their appeal to "friends and relatives . . . to respect the rights and privileges of your fellow Americans." And Hatcher added:

> There were numerous reports of whites going to the assistance of Negroes who found themselves at the mercy of white rioters and likewise there were numerous reports of Negroes going to the aid of whites who found themselves at the mercy of Negro rioters. These people are the real unsung heroes of the riot and Detroit should know that courage and decency did express themselves throughout the "nightmare."

In other words, as the *Free Press* later added editorially, "Detroit did not 'go to hell' completely."

8:30 P.M. The Mayor returned to the Police Commissioner's office and agreed with Police Superintendent Louis L. Berg that the situation was out of control.

The police were trying to drive back a crowd surging east on Vernor, intent on doing violence to the Negro ghetto centering in Paradise Valley. The white mob had been momentarily stopped at John R., a block east of Woodward. Milling, shouting, surging back and forth across Vernor Highway, the mob presented a horror-inspiring spectacle to Negroes in a hotel a block to the east. Then shots began to ring out through the stifling evening air. They seemed to be coming from the Frazer Hotel, a Negro hostelry on the southwest corner of Vernor Highway and Brush Street. This is the Detroit *News'* version of the affair:

One of the most serious of the shootings was at the Frazer Hotel, Vernor highway and Brush street.

Patrolman Lawrence Adams, of the Accident Prevention Bureau, was shot in the back and wounded seriously when he and Patrolman Howard Wickstrom, his partner, answered a riot call. A Negro fired on him as he was getting out of the A.P.B. car.

This was shortly after darkness fell. Adams' assailant was shot and killed.

A dozen more patrolmen arrived. Shots rang out from a dozen windows of the hotel and bullets began peppering the streets where the officers stood.

The police returned the fire, blazing away at windows in which partly concealed figures could be discerned. Tear gas bombs were hurled.

State police arrived and more Detroit police. Soon 50 officers were blazing away at the windows. The return fire from the hotel ceased.

A block away, at Vernor highway and John R. street, sniping began, with bullets coming from a three-story multiple dwelling. Officers poured round after round of bullets into the building. They fired more tear gas projectiles. Screams, smoke and occasional rifle fire presented a scene of din and confusion.

Nearly 1,000 spectators gathered and were dispersed with difficulty.

When firing from the building ceased, officers wearing white Office of Civilian Defense helmets entered with drawn pistols. The lights of the bullet-riddled structures began to be extinguished and finally they were in complete darkness. Dozens of Negroes were hustled off to hospitals and jails.

With a murderous mob howling for blood at their very doorsteps, some Negroes were seized with certain fear that their homes would be invaded. As a result, they resorted to the kind of random use of firearms one would expect from overwrought persons. This is the way in which the *Michigan Chronicle* gave this picture:

During the flareup at Brush and Vernor highway, one Negro, angered because the mob of whites had stoned his home, rushed out of the house and blazed away at them with a shot gun, scattering the mob. He was persuaded to return to his home by friends. . . .

Finally, after almost three hours, the police succeeded in dispersing the mob, which began a march down Vernor towards Woodward avenue.

Perhaps an hour later, Federal troops arrived.

8:40 P.M. Governor Kelly and Mayor Jeffries went to the office of Colonel Krech of the U. S. Army. Just before they arrived, Colonel Krech and other Army officers, looking into Fort Street from the Federal Building windows, saw a crowd of 500 white men pursuing a Negro on Fort Street from Woodward Avenue. The officers ran to the street and "rescued" the Negro, who by that time had been hammered into unconsciousness.

9 P.M. As darkness fell over the fear-smitten city, the disorders

assumed a more sinister aspect, or at least so they seemed. A *News* account highlighted this:

Eight policemen riding in a police cruiser and a scout car surprised a group of [Negro] men looting a grocery at 8246 Oakland avenue [north of the "Boulevards area"]. . . . Six of the policemen chased the men, while Patrolmen Alex Toncevitch and Riley Burton entered the store to investigate. Toncevitch carried a riot gun.

At the rear of the store, two men dived for the gun. Burton struck one with his fist. Toncevitch pulled the gun free, jumped back and sprayed the men with bullets.

One Negro . . . was killed instantly. The second Negro . . . was taken to Receiving Hospital in serious condition, his left side riddled.

A student overheard the following experience with looting:

I've had a store on Hastings Street [in Paradise Valley] for twenty years. I was always good to these people. During the depression, I ran up bills for them. I was like a father to them. Once I went down and got a woman's son out of jail for her.

So Monday, someone called me up at six in the morning and said, "Abe, don't come down today. . . . It's a bad riot." So I stayed home and listened to the police calls on the radio.

After dinner I hear come over the radio my store address. They're looting it through the back door. So I called up a colored woman, a customer who lives in an apartment across the street from my store. And I ask her, "Is it true?" And do you know what she says to me? She says, "Mister, don't bother me. Don't waste my time. My supper is getting cold."

9:05 P.M. Governor Kelly *informed* the commanding officer of District No. 1, Sixth Service Command, U. S. Army, that he would require the assistance of Federal troops to handle the Detroit situation. The 728th Military Police Battalion, which had first been put on the alert almost 18 hours earlier, at 3:30 a.m., was on its way to the intersection of Fort and Shelby, the Federal Building. But the Governor's request for Federal troops was still not in proper form.

9:25 P.M. Governor Kelly *made a formal official request* for Federal troops to the commander of the Sixth Service, Major General Aurand. Then, *twelve hours after the Governor's first request for Federal troops,* the 701st Military Police Battalion, which had been moved from Fort Custer to Fort Wayne during the day, was deployed to Fort Street and Woodward Avenue, and it moved up Woodward to disperse the crowds.

11 P.M. Informed that a proclamation from the President of the

United States was required if Federal troops were to be made available, Governor Kelly telephoned to Franklin D. Roosevelt and requested such a proclamation. . . .

"Well, they're off Woodward Avenue," Mayor Jeffries announced, "but I'm afraid not far off." He was referring to mobs of whites.

11:30 P.M. The Federal troops had the situation generally under control and quiet and order had been restored to the city.

11:55 P.M. President Roosevelt signed the proclamation requested by Governor Kelly calling upon the "military forces of the United States" to put down the "domestic violence" in Michigan. In traditional form, the President commanded "all persons engaged in said unlawful and insurrectionary proceedings to disperse and retire peaceably to their respective abodes immediately and hereafter abandon said combinations and submit themselves to the laws and constituted authorities of said state."

Almost fifteen hours had passed from the time that Governor Kelly had first made his telephone call to Chicago asking for Federal troops. And the major disorders were completely suppressed by the Federal soldiers *without firing a shot* half an hour before the President officially authorized them to act. *During the interval between the Governor's first request at 9 a.m. Monday morning and the entrance of the Federal troops into Detroit's riot areas Monday evening, irreparable damage had been done.*

A group of Negro soldiers stationed at Fort Custer, some hundred forty miles west of Detroit, in one of the quartermaster battalions, attempted to seize arms and a truck and start a pilgrimage to Detroit. "They wanted to go to Detroit to assist their families," Colonel Ralph Wiltamuth, post commander, said. "Prompt action by military authorities restored order. Five men are confined to the post stockade awaiting investigation."

SUMMARY: *Violence reached a peak during this period, with white mobs attempting to invade the Negro slum area called Paradise Valley. Police and Negro snipers fought a pitched battle in front of the Frazer Hotel on the edge of the Negro ghetto. Police were still shooting at Negro looters. At the same time as all this violence, a group of Negroes and whites met together in a settlement house to plan co-operation, and many whites and Negroes risked their own lives to save people of the other race from mobs of hoodlums. The Governor finally took the necessary steps to bring in the Federal troops. By midnight the*

*U. S. Army had established an "armed truce" between Detroit's war-
ring factions. A group of Negro soldiers at Fort Custer were arrested
in an attempt to take arms and a truck to assist their families in Detroit.*

TUESDAY, JUNE 22, 1943

Nor were the race riots finished on Monday. The peace was an
armed peace. Soldiers in jeeps and Army trucks, rifles on knees,
patrolled the streets. Some 6,000 Federal troops were bivouacked at
strategic points throughout the city, on high school play fields and
public library lawns. For the most part, eastside Negroes stayed in
their Paradise Valley district. This besieged ghetto also suffered from
a food shortage. A few Negroes sallied forth to work in the plants but
most were reluctant to leave their homes. They trusted the Federal
soldiers as they did not trust the City Police; but fear stalked them,
fear of the destruction of their homes and loved ones, of everything.

On Tuesday morning, Mayor Jeffries and Governor Kelly volubly
explained that the second phase of law enforcement had been reached.
The first phase was the difficult task of controlling and stopping the
riots. The second phase would now consist of the detection and pun-
ishment of those responsible for the disorder. The Governor's curfew
restrictions remained in force.

The City Courts began grinding out speedy justice to persons who
had been apprehended by the police, beginning with those arrested
in the early hours of the riots. . . . The Mayor gave assurances that no
worker need fear assault riding to and from his job. . . . Police Headquarters was barraged with fake telephone calls like those from the
real estate operator's friends the previous day. According to the Detroit
News, twelve of these fake calls came in a single hour:

> There was that report on Milwaukee and St. Aubin, for example. The
> woman who called said she saw it "with my own eyes." A white man had
> just been killed by a crowd of Negroes, she insisted. The squad car that
> rolled up to the intersection a few minutes later found a couple of girls
> playing hopscotch, and little else.

"The race rioting had subsided but people's imaginations have
not," a police dispatcher wearily remarked. . . .

But not all of the shooting was over. On Tuesday night, a Negro
was shot by a State Trooper. Two versions of this, the Witherspoon-
Anderson affair, provide a significant scene in the second day's disorders. For the purpose of contrast, two versions are given: one from

the Detroit *News,* that we call the *White Version;* and one from *The Racial Digest* for July, that we will call the *Negro Version.*

White Version:

Julian Witherspoon, Negro, . . . was wounded in the back by Theodore Anderson, of the State Troops, at the St. Antoine Y.M.C.A. . . .

Anderson and three policemen stopped three Negroes in an automobile at 11 p.m., to question them about the curfew violation. Anderson said that Witherspoon, watching from the sidewalk, began yelling, "Heil Hitler."

Anderson walked over to question Witherspoon. Witherspoon made a move toward his pocket, Anderson said. Anderson fired as Witherspoon reached the door of the Y.M.C.A.

Negro Version:

At 8 p.m. several men were playing softball on the sidewalk in front of the St. Antoine Y.M.C.A. As the police passed one of the boys was told to get his G— D— off the streets. We don't give a G— D— whom we shoot tonight. At 10:05 William Reid saw Julian Witherspoon enter the Y.M.C.A. door. An officer jumped out of a state police car, ran towards the Y.M.C.A. door, raised his gun and shot through the glass in the door, hitting Witherspoon. He was reported by the police as having said "Heil Hitler" to them.

Witherspoon staggered up the steps and fell in the lobby. The officers entered and lined other men, including the desk clerk, with their faces toward the wall, after clubbing and beating them. The police searched desk drawers and locker rooms. They threw out NAACP [National Association for the Advancement of Colored People] literature saying, "Here's something to read," as if in fun.

David Morgan, one of the men, looked around. An officer walked over and asked him, "What in the G— D— are you looking at?" and slapped him.

The officers called the men black bastards, apes, sons of ——. George Haynes who had come downstairs from his room upon hearing the commotion was also lined up against the wall. He remarked, "It is a shame we law-abiding citizens have to be treated like Fascists." The officer struck him with his club.

A Sheaffer fountain pen was taken from one of them. Before searching the men one officer said "Shoot any of them that move because we have plenty of bullets left, and you'll get the same thing as your buddy." The officers did not find as much as a pen knife on any of the men.

One trooper asked, "Is he [Witherspoon] dead yet?" The reply was "No." One officer walked over toward him and said to his companion, "Don't forget to say he pulled a gun."

There was no attempt made to get medical aid for Witherspoon until 5 minutes before the officers left. He was on the floor for forty minutes.

Despite this harrowing event, the city had returned to a greater semblance of normality by Tuesday night. A crowd of 800 who assembled in a park across the street from Northeastern High School, in a Polish-American section, were dispersed, but with some difficulty. Rumors and reports of occasional sluggings and of rocks and bullets crashing through streetcar windows continued to circulate, but the "armed truce" was taking hold.

SUMMARY: *Most Negroes were afraid to leave their homes in Paradise Valley and go to work in the plants of the "Arsenal of Democracy." Provocative rumors and fake telephone calls persisted. A State Trooper shot a Negro through the door of the Negro Y.M.C.A. The armed peace was in force.*

WEDNESDAY, JUNE 23, 1943

R. J. Thomas, President of the United Automobile Workers' Union (C.I.O.) issued an eight-point program of "immediate and effective community action" to forestall a recurrence of race riots in Detroit. His proposals were characterized the following morning by the *Free Press* as "not only timely but specific and they treat of longterm as well as immediate causes of mobocracy." The *Free Press* "indorses each one of them" and said that Thomas "was the only Detroiter who had come forward with a set of formal recommendations looking toward a restoration of inter-racial accord for our riot-ravaged city."

R. J. Thomas called for (1) a special grand jury to investigate causes, (2) adequate park and recreation facilities, (3) new housing plans for Negro slum areas, (4) effective curbs on racial intolerance and discrimination in industrial relations, (5) investigation of why more drastic action to subdue the mobs had not been taken earlier, (6) impartial justice to the rioters, regardless of color, (7) restitution of losses to innocent sufferers from the reign of terror, and (8) "Creation by the Mayor of a special bi-racial committee of 10 to make further recommendations looking toward elimination of racial differences and friction." To this last he added, "This committee will have a special job in connection with our high schools, where racial hatred has been permitted to grow and thrive in recent years."

The last attempt at violence in Detroit's Bloody Week had been foreshadowed by the threatened riot the previous night in front of Northeastern High School, and it was precipitated by a typical evidence of American democracy: the graduation of 29 Negroes as a part of the Class of 1943 from that school! Since a debate arose as to the actual events of that Wednesday evening, it will be well to set forth

first the following account by Lyford Moore, Detroit *Free Press* staff
writer, based upon his own observations:

At a commencement somewhat abbreviated to assure the . . . graduates
of getting home before the ten o'clock curfew, Walter P. Reuther . . . told
the class that it was the "most tragic thing I know . . . that . . . armored cars
are patrolling the streets of Detroit with guns made here in the arsenal of
democracy." . . .

Principal Charles M. Novak's parting words . . . warned them seriously
not to loiter . . . for congratulations . . .

Eight members of a military police battalion had kept peace in the
auditorium. In the park beyond, 80 policemen were stationed to prevent a
recurrence of the previous night's rioting.

The class . . . went out of the building at 9:15 p.m.—into the world they
had talked of, and the 29 Negroes almost at once learned something of one
of the problems that must be solved before democracy can be saved.

In the park stood clusters of other [white] youths, ringed by officers
ceaselessly patrolling. As the graduates emerged, the hoodlums slowly and
by clusters commenced moving closer to the curb.

Before your eyes, what had been 200 youths was transformed into a
mob. As an ocean wave flows . . . past the piling . . . so came the rioters
through the ranks of the policemen.

Now there were easily 400—and they were between the [Negro] graduates and the policemen. . . .

Five Negro boys emerged from the building in a body and turned east.
Instantly the pulsating mob . . . began moving in the same direction. By the
time the Negroes had crossed the street at the corner, the entire parkway
between the curb and the sidewalk and all the yards in the block were
filled with the mob. . . .

Behind or beside each policeman . . . little islands of trembling Negroes
formed. . . .

Suddenly shouting started a block away from the building and policemen . . . raced to the spot. In another instant the pressure would have
broken the dam, for the 30 to 40 policemen . . . appeared woefully small
against a block crammed with snarling hoodlums.

Then, from around a corner, four truckloads of soldiers with bayonetted
rifles appeared. . . . Only seconds later they had dismounted and formed a
khaki corral around the mob threatening to break over the curb.

Slowly then, bayonets only inches away from the bellies of the rioters,
they peeled the unhealthy rind away from the black graduates.

Marching five abreast in the street, they drove the rioters back . . .
beyond the school.

The Police Commissioner, John H. Witherspoon, did not understand it
that way. He said that there were no arrests and that no one tried to
incite a riot there. The Detroit *News* the following afternoon quoted
the Commissioner as follows:

The Chene Precinct report shows that at 6 p.m. 20 police officers and several scout cars and cruisers were at the school. . . . At 9:10 p.m., when the graduation exercises ended, there was a crowd of several hundred persons across the street in Perrien Park.

From 50 to 60 youths between the ages of 15 and 20 were in the vicinity and when the graduates and their friends came out, about 20 of the youths followed them. The police went along.

Simultaneously, two truckloads of soldiers came up and their commanding officer inquired why the crowd had gathered. Police explained that graduation exercises had ended.

There was no fixing of bayonets by the soldiers, as reported, and they continued on their way. By 9:30 everyone had left the vicinity.

Charles M. Novak, Principal of Northeastern High School stated, "There was a large crowd in the auditorium and in the streets, but I saw no disorder or violence." However, Walter P. Reuther, Vice-President of the United Automobile Workers' Union (C.I.O.), who spoke at the graduation exercises, verified Lyford Moore's account in a statement published in the Friday morning *Free Press*.

SUMMARY: *R. J. Thomas, President of the United Automobile Workers' Union (C.I.O.), issued an eight-point program for the promotion of inter-racial peace. Twenty-nine Negro members of the Class of 1943, Northeastern High School, faced a near race riot as they left their graduation exercises. The U. S. Army provided them with safe conduct.*

Negroes had been afraid to come out of the eastside section to buy food, and the Emergency Relief Division of the Office of Civilian Defense, under the direction of Mrs. Beulah T. Whitby, opened up relief offices in several of the eastside schools. But this was not necessary for long. Merchants began to restock their looted food stores; Negro men became willing to leave their families and return to work; and the city started to ponder *who, what, and why.*

AND THEN WHAT HAPPENED?
CHRONOLOGY CONCLUDED

"**L**ET us face the fact that . . . racial antagonism exists, and that it is deep-rooted," W. K. Kelsey—the Detroit *News'* clear-eyed "Commentator"—told his fellow-citizens. "Still, it does not excuse rioting." And he added,

There are thousands of whites who resent the claims of the Negro to social and even industrial equality. There are thousands of Negroes who resent the discrimination which makes it so hard for them to obtain, or having obtained, to keep employment among white workers, commensurate with their ability. . . .

The remarkable feature of the post-riot cases before the courts is the youth of so many of the defendants. . . . Religious and racial antagonism is not born in them; it is inculcated, and it is inculcated neither in the schools nor in the churches, but in the home and on the street. . . .

Those responsible, then, for Monday's riots . . . will not go to jail. It is not illegal to teach intolerance and hatred.

Nor is it "illegal" to proceed after race riots in such a way that unhealed wounds are allowed to fester and become rancoring sores. As New York's *PM* put it, in connection with Harlem's Negro riots of August 1 and 2, 1943, whites should remember that "the club of the policeman wherever he may be, Beaumont or Detroit or Birmingham, falls not upon one victim alone. It falls upon a race. The bell tolls for all."

The Detroit "armed truce" gradually simmered down to more peaceful conditions by Thursday morning, but an undercurrent of terror remained. A young Negro housewife living in the riot zone voiced this dread on Thursday, as follows:

The situation is in hand a little better but there was a man shot right around here yesterday [Wednesday]. When the Army leaves, it will be rioting worse than ever unless the Army waits a long time to leave.
A Negro mail carrier put it this way:

It's under control now, but for how long? Somebody called the wife of the head of the NAACP [National Association for the Advancement of Colored People]—it was a Negro woman who called—and said that a white man at the plant where her husband worked had told him that they were just laying down until this thing quieted down and the troops left town and then they were coming over here [the North End] and burn us out of this section of town.

This last was obviously a scare-rumor, the sort of rumor that prepares minds for new race riots. But let us follow the chronology of events further. Let us see what steps were taken to treat Detroit's race riot wounds.

THURSDAY, JUNE 24, 1943

On the third day after Bloody Monday, Governor Kelly decided to ease curfew restrictions. He made midnight the street curfew; permitted alcoholic beverages to be sold between 7 a.m. and 10 p.m.; allowed later closing hours for places of amusement; and reopened Belle Isle to recreation seekers. He cancelled in addition all emergency regulations as they affected the adjoining Counties of Oakland and Macomb.

Several inquiries were started, and Congressman Dies threatened to start one of his own. The Governor appointed a fact-finding committee of public officials and called for an early report from them. And Dr. Lowell S. Selling, head of the Recorder's Court Psychiatric Clinic of Detroit, assisted by his entire staff of 23 psychiatrists, clinical assistants, and clerks, began an inquiry into the mental condition of 1,000 rioters. Announcing at the outset the kinds of "psychopathic failings" he expected to uncover, Dr. Selling said that "with 30 to 35 minutes to a person" he hoped to have a picture of the situation in "a few days at most." In addition to those two lines of inquiry, the Honorable Martin Dies of Texas, a Congressman from a district in which Negroes have traditionally "failed to qualify" to vote and the Chairman of the House Committee on Un-American Activities, threatened to descend upon Detroit and conduct a hearing into the causes of the race riots. As usual, Dies had an *a priori* basis for his investigations: He had the idea that the riots were fomented by Japanese-Americans who had been legally released from internment camps on the west coast after

having been certified to the satisfaction of the U. S. Army as safely
"pro-American." With the exception of the Rev. Gerald L. K. Smith and
a few of his kind, Detroit newspapers and civic leaders joined in asking Dies to stay away from Detroit. They did not want a bad
situation further confused with prejudiced and discredited investigating methods. . . .

The first meeting to form a permanent inter-racial citizens' body
took place in the evening, at the Redeemer Presbyterian Church, in
answer to a call by Dr. Benjamin J. Bush, President of the Detroit
Council of Churches. This was later to be named the Greater Detroit
Inter-Racial Fellowship, and was to embrace all possible race, religious,
labor, nationality, and other groups. Plans for the creation of this body
had been in the making ever since the Sojourner Truth Homes race
riots, but it was not until the week before Bloody Monday that the
June 24 meeting had been scheduled.

At this meeting, the body unanimously adopted the first seven of
R. J. Thomas's eight points. The newly-formed organization refused to
accept Thomas's eighth point, that an inter-racial committee be
appointed by the Mayor, because—as someone at the meeting asserted
—an official Mayor's committee would be hamstrung in its work by all
kinds of political pressures and fears.

The Nazi-controlled Vichy radio hailed the Detroit riots as a
"revolt" that would spread to other cities, a reflection of "the moral and
social crisis in the United States." It piously added, "Today, on the
morrow of the bloody incidents of Detroit, the French people, imbued
with a sense of social justice, realize the dangers for European civilization inherent in the American aims of world domination." . . .
Maximum misdemeanor penalties—90 days in the Detroit House of
Correction—were meted out to several groups of rioters.

FRIDAY, JUNE 25, 1943

The Governor's fact-finding committee issued its first report. After
several conferences with officers of law enforcing agencies, the
committee concluded that sufficient evidence did not exist to indicate
that the riots had resulted from organized instigation. It therefore
arrived at the following startling *non-sequitur:* that the situation did
not warrant a special grand jury. The grand jury, at any rate, was not
ordered. . . .

Mayor Jeffries appointed a twelve-member inter-racial committee to study the race situation. As chairman, he appointed William J. Norton, Executive Vice-President of the Children's Fund of Michigan, and the members were five other whites and six Negroes. . . .

At the request of the Governor, Dr. C. F. Ramsey, Director of the State Department of Social Welfare, began what the newspapers called a "sociological inquiry" into the background of several hundred police prisoners picked up in the race riots. . . .

The Detroit Council of Churches, through its President, the Rev. Dr. Benjamin J. Bush, called upon the people of Detroit to observe the following Sunday as a day of humility and penitence. . . .

Funeral services were held for some of the riot victims. . . . Officials tried once more to quiet rumors that as many as 400 persons had died in the race clashes, but the unsubstantiated rumor persisted.

SATURDAY, JUNE 26, 1943

Detroit remained "on probation" over the weekend. The Governor decided not to relax further the restrictions promulgated by him six days before. . . . The Inter-Racial Citizens' Committee, dating from the time of the Sojourner Truth race riots early in 1942 and headed by Pastor Hill, asked Mayor Jeffries to discourage the announced plan of Congressman Dies to come to Detroit for an inquiry. . . . Mayor Jeffries asked Police Commissioner Witherspoon to send a message over the police teletype to the effect that "the riot is over and the Police Department is to return to normal."

SUNDAY, JUNE 27, 1943

The city was abnormally quiet that Sunday. Some 500 white and 200 Negro families visited Belle Isle where a week before estimates had placed the total at 100,000, of whom possibly 85 percent were colored. . . . Governor Kelly made this statement on the question of troop removal: "I must know that Detroit will be assured of adequate manpower at any further outbreak of racial trouble before I will ask for the troops' withdrawal." . . . Ministers offered prayers for peace and harmony in hundreds of Detroit's churches. . . . Paradise Valley merchants sorted over materials police had recovered from looters.

MONDAY, JUNE 28, 1943

Just short of one week after his declaration of a state of emergency, Governor Kelly lifted virtually all restrictions on civilians.

Bottled liquor, however, was not to be sold. Federal troops were to remain for at least another week, and during this time they were to give training to the relatively green Michigan State Troops which had been organized to replace the National Guard units taken into the U. S. Army.

The Mayor's Inter-Racial Committee convened and agreed to center its efforts on the reduction of race frictions rather than to attempt to fix the blame for the riots.

The daily newspapers carried stories based upon a "Statement Unanimously Adopted by the Executive Board, Detroit Chapter, National Lawyers' Guild on the Recent Disorders in Detroit." This candid analysis of the situation concluded that the "charges of mismanagement laid at the door of the police commissioner plainly require investigation." It also called for the creation of "a commission on the development of inter-racial accord in Detroit to consist of three white and three Negro members," the endowment of "such a commission with authority to compel testimony by subpoena and to administer oaths," and the appropriation initially of a sum of $100,000 to subsidize its efforts.

Police Commissioner John H. Witherspoon himself made a report to City Council, a kind of "white paper," in which he not only vindicated the police, their policies, and their activities in connection with the riot, but praised the police as having shown "rare courage and efficiency" in handling the matter. The Commissioner pointed out that early violent rioting occurred in the Negro sections of the city's east side and that white "retaliatory action" had then speedily followed. He defended the so-called "kid gloves" policy enjoined by the Mayor upon the Police Department. As the Commissioner put it,

We are at war—this was not believed to be a proper time, with a mailed-fist policy, to attempt to solve a racial conflict and a basic antagonism which has been growing and festering for years.

Such a policy could well have precipitated a race riot at a much earlier date and one of much more serious proportions. The fact remains that this department did not precipitate the riot.

Some have advocated a "shoot-to-kill" policy. Such a procedure might have terminated the riot at an earlier hour, but I am sure that it would have been with a far greater loss of life. . . .

If a "shoot-to-kill" policy was right, my judgment was wrong.

The alternatives were thus set in the Commissioner's mind between the alleged "kid gloves" policy his department was said to have followed and a "shoot-to-kill" policy. Many would see at least one other course.

City Councilman George C. Edwards tried to bring the discussions of his colleagues down to earth and into a somewhat more constructive and less apologetic vein by offering a practical six-point program. He proposed: (1) that the Governor call a 23-man county grand jury, charged especially with inquiry into the fifteen unsolved murders; (2) that City Council help Mayor Jeffries keep the Dies Un-American Committee out of town; (3) that the possibility of subversive activities be investigated thoroughly; (4) that the Federal troops be kept as long as possible and arrangements made "for their speedy mobilization if needed again"; (5) that the Police Commissioner "appoint 200 Negro policemen for duty in Negro areas, if this is possible under the competitive examinations for policemen"; and (6) that the City Council set up a committee to work with the Mayor's Committee on Inter-Racial Relations, "with emphasis on added recreational and housing facilities for Negroes."

TUESDAY, JUNE 29, 1943

The City Council rejected nearly all of Councilman Edward's program. Council members joined with Police Commissioner Witherspoon in opposing the grand jury proposal. The Commissioner pointed out that all investigating agencies had searched the facts and that "none has one shred of proof now that the riot was planned or inspired." To this, he added these other protestations:

Possibly at some later date such evidence will develop and a grand jury could be called. . . . I have no objection to a grand jury. It would be an easy out for me. Don't get the impression I'm afraid of a grand jury. But it would be an unfair position to put any judge in.

This strange logic did not convince Councilman Edwards. To simplify matters, he withdrew all of his suggestions except the ones that a grand jury be called and that City Council appoint a committee on race relations. By a formal vote, City Council rejected the proposal for a 23-man grand jury and approved that for a City Council committee. As a result, Council President John Lodge appointed a five-man committee charged with the responsibility for planning and financing new housing, recreation facilities, and other improvements to relieve pressure in the overcrowded sections of the city. . . .

The Detroit Branch of the National Association for the Advancement of Colored People sent a list of recommendations to Mayor Jeffries. They urged: (1) a grand jury investigation of the Police

Department [an eventuality Commissioner Witherspoon apparently feared]; (2) extension of recreational facilities; (3) the hiring of more Negro school teachers; (4) removal of racial restrictions on all public housing units; (5) opening of summer camps to the children of all races.

WEDNESDAY, JUNE 30, 1943

Mayor Jeffries issued his "white paper," as the newspapers called it, to City Council on Wednesday, June 30. He explained in detail why it took so long for him to obtain the aid of State and Federal troops and admitted that much of the responsibility for bloodshed rested upon the long hours of delay in making final arrangements to get military aid. Here are some high points from the Mayor's statement:

It took us 24 hours to establish the peace after rioting broke out on the Belle Isle bridge the night of June 20. It took us 12 hours to get the Federal troops on the scene. . . .

It will not take us that long next time, and . . . you have my guarantee on that. . . .

We knew there was a full battalion of military police . . . stationed at Rouge Park. It was our understanding that it was ready to move instantly upon orders. . . .

That was our understanding because there had been many, many discussions over at least a period of a year on how to get the regular Army troops here in any emergency situation. . . .

But now you know that despite all of these discussions, despite Col. Krech's practice tests with the troops, despite his precautions, that the formula for getting the Army troops here quickly broke down for one reason and for one reason alone. We . . . could not get the necessary Army order to pry the troops loose when we wanted it.

Mayor Jeffries covered his position on a crucial point when he said he objected to outright martial law because "civil functions would be completely abrogated and the Army commander in charge would rule the area exclusively." He warmly praised the Police Department, saying that its "role in the riot needs no defense. On the whole it was splendid and at times magnificent." He was "rapidly losing . . . patience with those Negro leaders who insisted that their people do not and will not trust policemen and the Police Department. After what happened I am certain that some of these leaders are more vocal in their caustic criticism of the Police Department than they are in educating their own people to their responsibilities as citizens."

The Mayor's "was a fine statement," observed Councilman Comstock, "but it won't settle the racial question in Detroit. Nothing will

settle that. The racial conflict has been going on in this country since
our ancestors made the first mistake of bringing the Negroes to this
country." The Councilman bespoke the trend of sentiment among a
sizable segment of Detroit's white citizenry. Councilman Edwards,
with his insistence upon curative measures, represented another—probably larger—segment.

Mayor Jeffries also assured the East Side Merchants Association
that they should re-open the rest of their stores, and that they could
expect "not only protection, but better police protection than you have
ever had." The association is composed of the white owners of stores
in the eastside Negro area. . . . The renewed disquietude of the
merchants had arisen from an episode in which four unidentified
hoodlums raced through the streets of northwest Detroit in a red
sedan hurling bricks through the windows of cars and houses.

THURSDAY, JULY 1, 1943

Editorial commendation for Mayor Jeffries' "white paper" was
somewhat offset by a letter of protest on it sent to the Mayor and the
newspapers by James J. McClendon, M.D., President of the Detroit
Chapter, National Association for the Advancement of Colored People.

We do not condone the acts of hoodlums of our race [Dr. McClendon
stated], any more than you condone those who overturned cars . . . on
Woodward avenue. . . .
It takes no crystal gazer to add the number of Negroes slain by the
police or compare the lack of such "shoot to kill" policy on Woodward
avenue. . . .
Killings, vile name-calling, wanton, unnecessary arrests of colored citizens, inspired no regard for a Police Department which spoke of some of
our citizens as "niggers." . . .
In 1941, you appointed a Mayor's Committee after the Northwestern
High School Riot. The committee . . . studied the conflict situation. Its
recommendations were laid upon your desk where they lie today, un-
heeded. . . .
Today we have a new committee. Its report can be written now. The
question is whether you will do anything about it. . . .

Patrolman Lawrence A. Adams, shot in the race rioting on June 21,
died in Harper Hospital. . . .
Police Commissioner Witherspoon told the Mayor's Bi-Racial
Committee that new Negro policemen could be added to the force only
through the usual competitive civil service examinations. He added

that he would like to augment the Negro detail if it were possible. He tried to leave no doubt that he intended to punish any policeman found guilty of reviling Negroes, but he insisted that some of the names Negroes reserved for policemen were even nastier than those policemen were alleged to employ on Negroes.

The Mayor's Bi-Racial Committee also gave consideration to the housing problem and heard Brigadier General Thomas Colladay's defense of the conduct of the Michigan State Troops. "It was our first big mobilization," he pointed out. "Mobilization of volunteers takes more time than for soldiers." . . .

With the tentative approval of Commissioner Witherspoon, Inspector John O. Whitman, head of the City Homicide Squad, sought through County Prosecutor Dowling and the Wayne County Board of Auditors to post rewards of $50 for information which would lead to the solution of thirteen unsolved riot deaths. . . . The Rev. Gerald L. K. Smith, whom the late Huey Long praised as "a better rabble-rouser" than he was, made this disclaimer:

The thought that I had anything to do with the Detroit race riot is almost too ridiculous to entertain, and the accusation is almost too extreme to answer.

FRIDAY, JULY 2, 1943

The Rev. Horace White, Negro member of the Detroit Housing Commission, called for the inclusion of 1,000 new dwelling units in the Negro slum districts as a part of a project to erect 3,000 new dwellings with funds allocated to the National Housing Agency. The Commission adopted the proposal and ordered that it be carried out at sites in the Negro districts.

SUNDAY, JULY 4, 1943

Lieutenant Governor Eugene C. Keyes stated that the main reason State Troops had not assisted earlier in the race riots on June 21 was that they were not *properly* requested. . . . The County Board of Auditors was asked by Prosecutor Dowling to post rewards of $100 (rather than $50) for information leading to the conviction of persons guilty of each of thirteen unsolved riot deaths.

MONDAY, JULY 5, 1943

Governor Kelly announced that Federal troops would remain in Wayne County until at least August 2. This would have the advantage

of providing a longer period in which to continue the training and
organization of the Michigan State Troops. Federal troops, meanwhile,
ceased their street patrols. On Monday evening, after marching in
regimental formation up Woodward Avenue, Federal and State troops
massed in solid phalanx in front of a reviewing stand before the Detroit Institute of Arts and heard warm words of praise for their efforts
from Major General Henry S. Aurand, in command of the Federal
soldiers.

WEDNESDAY, JULY 7, 1943

In his first formal statement on the Detroit race riots, Governor
Kelly explained that it was not until 11 p.m. on June 21 (Bloody
Monday) that he became aware that a signed proclamation by Presi-
dent Roosevelt was necessary for the use of the Federal troops.

Upon arrival at Detroit [the Governor stated]: I . . . went to the 6th
Army Corps Command at Detroit to confer in regard to Federal assistance. . . .
This conference was brought to a sudden . . . conclusion when the
commanding Federal officer . . . received word from his superior officer . . .
that the Federal assistance could not be given unless . . . I would declare
the necessity for . . . Federal martial law. . . .
I informed the Federal authorities that the situation at that time did
not make it possible for me to declare the necessity of such drastic action. . . .
About 8:30 that evening I received word from the District Command
Office . . . that they had found out that my request could be granted without the necessity of a declaration of Federal martial law. . . .
It was approximately 9:00 o'clock that night . . . when I did sign the
formal request . . . and I was there informed . . . that that was all that
was necessary. . . .
I proceeded on an hour-and-a-half tour of the city, returning to the
Police Headquarters shortly before 11 o'clock.
Upon my return I was informed . . . for the first time that . . . the commanding officers of Detroit and Chicago did not possess the power to move
troops without a presidential proclamation. . . .
I immediately placed that call to the President.
He [the President] informed me that the proclamation had not yet
reached him, but was on the way, and that he . . . wanted to be sure that
the Federal troops would move into the Detroit area, assisting the constituted authorities, and without a declaration of Federal martial law.
When the Army moved in they did a mighty fine job.

Donald Van Zile, Presiding Judge of the Recorder's Court, denied
blanket re-trials to those convicted of riot participation shortly after
the cessation of overt hostilities. Pastor White had requested the re-

trials on the ground that in the "heat of the tragedy" the judges had become "frightened like the rest of us" and had lost their sense of legal equilibrium. "I wish to say," replied Judge Van Zile, "that at no time were any of the judges frightened, nor did they lose their equilibrium."

FRIDAY, JULY 9, 1943

The city had gone back to something that was being called "normalcy," a term reminiscent of President Warren G. Harding and of a similar era after another and much larger war. . . . Advised by James R. Walsh, Assistant City Corporation Counsel, that the City of Detroit had no legal liability for damages suffered by its citizens during the race riots, the City Council set a hearing for the following Thursday (July 15) on a claim by a white Brush Street grocer for $9,000, the value of his entire stock looted or destroyed during the riots. . . . Governor Kelly expressed thanks to the Detroit social workers who had conducted investigative interviews among the arrested rioters.

SATURDAY, JULY 10, 1943

Of the more than 4,000 soldiers who had been sent in to quell the race riots, only 1,400 soldiers in two Military Police Battalions remained in the city. Detroit was again designated as "in bounds" for Fort Custer soldiers.

MONDAY, JULY 12, 1943

John S. Bugas, Special Agent in charge of the Detroit F.B.I. office, spoke before the Michigan Association of Chiefs of Police who were holding a war conference at Charlevoix. He asserted that the Detroit police did a "magnificent and heroic job" in the race riots.

TUESDAY, JULY 13, 1943

A white rioter, George Miller, 31, a convicted counterfeiter and larcenist, was sentenced to 90 days in the Detroit House of Correction. Miller was identified from a news photograph that showed two Detroit policemen holding a Negro victim and Miller brazenly slapping the Negro. Detective John J. Richard recognized Miller in the photograph and arrested him in a saloon hangout. Patrolman

Paul Gyslvic, one of the officers in the picture, said that Miller was not arrested on the spot because he and his fellow officer had their hands full taking care of the mauled and stabbed Negro. . . .

Pastor White, the Negro leader, released a report compiled by Sheridan A. Bruseaux, a Chicago private investigator, which ascribed the riots largely to inadequate housing and poor recreational facilities.

THURSDAY, JULY 15, 1943

Attorney General Francis Biddle sent a letter to President Roosevelt on July 15 that was published in full August 10 in the *American Labor News*, supplement for shop papers issued by the United Automobile Workers (C.I.O.). Although the paper did not indicate how it had come by this confidential document, New York's *PM* also printed it.

In this letter, the Attorney General summarized the results of conferences by his personal representative with Governor Kelly, Mayor Jeffries, Police Commissioner Witherspoon, and other officials, the observations of Monsignor Haas of the Federal Fair Employment Practice Committee, and "daily reports from the Federal Bureau of Investigation." The letter contains these particularly significant passages:

All of those familiar with the situation agree on the causes of the riot; briefly they may be summarized as follows:

There is no evidence of any Axis, or Fascist, or Ku Klux Klan incitement. In fact there is no evidence of any concerted action to bring about the riots. From the enclosed report to me from Mr. Rhetts, who represented me in Detroit, it is evident that the trouble started on Belle Isle, where there was a crowd on Sunday night, June 20th, of approximately 100,000 persons, of which 90 per cent were colored. The prevailing hostility between sailors and Negroes inflamed the Detroit riot in its first stages when sailors from the Navy Arsenal near the end of the Belle Isle bridge joined in the fights. Rioting spread late in the evening to the colored district along Hastings Street, known as Paradise Valley, where the overcrowding is very bad. Many Negroes were shot as a result of the looting. . . .

The causes of the riots are apparent. During the past three years the population of Detroit has increased by 485,000 people, many of whom are colored. There are no subways or elevated trains in Detroit so that the transportation situation is particularly difficult causing great overcrowding in the buses. The housing situation, particularly among the colored sections, is deplorable. The same is true of the recreation situation, which is greatly overburdened and overcrowded.

The Detroit Police Department is, in spite of the increase in population, actually 280 men short of budget allotment. Moreover, many of the present policemen are not well trained on account of the number of men who have been drafted and whose places had to be filled from the only available and often inadequate personnel. These conditions prevail generally throughout the country.

Much of the violence could have been prevented had the troops arrived sooner. It is believed that there was a misunderstanding between the local officials and the military as to what steps should be taken to arrange for the troops to come in.

It is extremely interesting that there was no disorder WITHIN PLANTS, where colored and white men worked side by side, on account of efficient union discipline.

I believe that the riots in Detroit do not represent an isolated case but are typical of what may occur in other cities throughout the country. The situation in Los Angeles is extremely tense; I am also concerned with the racial unrest in Washington, D. C., Chicago, Ill., and elsewhere. The hot season up to Labor Day, when crowds seek outdoor relief, is the period of greatest danger.

As a result of such findings, Biddle believed "that certain steps could be taken which would, to a certain extent, ameliorate similar conditions elsewhere." He therefore recommended these six steps:

1. That you suggest to the Secretary of War that he work out a simple manual in co-operation with the Department of Justice which could be used by all local officials and by corps commanders to expedite the procedure of sending in troops.

2. That you suggest to Mr. McNutt that immediate arrangements be made to defer members of the city police forces. [In this connection he quoted F.B.I. Chief J. Edgar Hoover to the point that failure to make such deferments would lead to "a repetition of internal disorders such as the Los Angeles 'zoot suit' cases and the Detroit race riots."] . . .

3. That careful consideration be given to limiting, and in some instances putting an end to, Negro migrations into communities which cannot absorb them, either on account of their physical limitations or cultural background. This needs immediate and careful consideration. When postwar readjustments begin, and jobs are scarcer, the situation will become far more acute. Witness the dislocations in cities caused by the migrations shortly after the last world war. It would seem pretty clear that no more Negroes should move to Detroit. Yet I know of no controls being considered or exercised. You might wish to have the recommendations of Mr. McNutt as to what could and should be done.

4. As to the general situation, I suggest that you direct the organization of an inter-departmental committee . . . to exchange information and discuss policies. Responsibility so far as possible should be fixed in the Committee to co-ordinate information work in this field and deal with delegations who have been coming to Washington to see you. . . .

5. I think it would be advisable that a national committee be formed to

make a study of the whole situation and do an extended educational and publicity job chiefly in the local communities. Obviously this is something that the Government cannot do nor do I think you should appoint such a committee. . . .

6. It has been suggested that you should go on the radio to discuss the whole problem. This, I think, would be unwise. However, you might consider discussing it the next time you talk about the overall domestic situation as one of the problems to be considered.

When the third Biddle recommendation was challenged as contrary to the Federal Constitution by Lester B. Granger, Executive Secretary, National Urban League, the Attorney General replied that he could not comment on his "strictly confidential" letter to the President, but he did express his views on Negro migration. He pointed to the difficulty cities were having in absorbing large numbers of war workers, whether Negro or white, and said:

It seems to me advisable, therefore, that responsible officials should give careful consideration to the extent of required facilities before taking any steps to fill the particular manpower requirements.

Many of the Attorney General's conclusions strengthen observations reported in the foregoing chronology, especially in Chapter 3. It will also be observed that his recommendation of a governmental and a non-governmental set of twin organizations for handling racial problems suggests on a nationwide scale what Chapter 10 urges in each locality with a large Negro population. But Biddle did not suggest a *bi-racial* commission, and he did not urge a *bi-racial* civic body. On the contrary, the segregative impression one gains from his third recommendation is further strengthened in his fourth and fifth recommendations. And this is the attitude to which Granger and other exponents of inter-racial co-operation immediately took exception. It is the glaring and dangerous defect of Biddle's whole report.

*   *   *   *

For a time after the issuance of the Bruseaux report on July 13, nothing of significance took place locally that bore on the causes of the riots or on steps to prevent their recurrence. The general feeling of the white citizenry seemed to be that the less said about the whole affair the better off everyone would be.

One ex-felon, Robert Morgan, a convicted white slaver, easily identifiable in several news photos (one reproduced on the jacket of this book) in the act of assaulting a Negro, was momentarily freed because police could find no complainant to appear against him. One of the victims of his depredations subsequently came to the fore and made a formal complaint.

The Negro population still frankly lacked confidence in the police. This feeling was augmented by what it regarded as unwarranted arrests and the ruthless search of private homes for riot loot without due process of law.

The Mayor's Bi-Racial Committee, save for the recommendation by a sub-committee for a grand jury, continued to "muddle through" in much the same well-intentioned fashion that it had begun its work. The problems of housing and recreation, mentioned by so many investigators as basic factors in the riot outbreaks, were receiving only desultory consideration by the agencies charged with taking definite steps to solve such problems. Detroit had largely gotten back to its "business as usual" method of ignoring its social problems when several new events again focused attention upon "doing something about it."

* * * *

Gerald L. K. Smith continued his agitation of racial intolerance with an article on "Race Riots!" in the July number of his organ, *The Cross and the Flag*, published late in July. He gives his ideas on how to handle Negroes, as follows:

I know of no self-respecting person in the City of Detroit who is opposed to Negroes having every modern facility necessary to make them comfortable and to assist them in their desire to be progressive. BUT . . . Most white people will not agree to any of the following suggestions:

1. Inter-marriage of blacks and whites.
2. Mixture of blacks and whites in hotels.
3. Mixture of blacks and whites in restaurants.
4. Intimate relationships between blacks and whites in the school system.
5. Wholesale mixture of blacks and whites in residential sections.
6. Promiscuous mixture of blacks and whites in street cars and on trains, especially where black men are permitted to sit down and crowd in close to white women and vice versa. I have every reason to believe black women resent being crowded by white men on street cars and elsewhere.
7. Promiscuous mixture of blacks and whites in factories, especially where black men are mixed with white women closely in daily work.

Following the riots, fourteen national organizations had appealed to the Department of Justice to seek the indictment of Smith in connection with the outbreaks. His 100% white authoritarian point of view

reminds one quite grimly of Nazi and Fascist ideology, of Southern
Ku Klux Klanism at its worst.

SATURDAY, JULY 24, 1943

One event that may have joggled Detroit a bit was the "CBS
Open Letter on Race Hatred" broadcast over the Columbia Broad-
casting System's network at 7 to 7:30 p.m. this Saturday and repeated
at 9 to 9:30 p.m. Particularly striking was the dramatized letter's
"postscript" by Wendell L. Willkie in which he spoke of the "situation
which flared so tragically in Detroit" and which "has its counterpart—
actual or potential—in many American cities." He added that such
"instances of mob-madness cannot be treated as single cases, because
they are profound in their effect in this country and lasting in their
impression throughout the world." He scored particularly the basic
motivation of race rioters, "the same basic motivation as actuates the
fascist mind when it seeks to dominate whole peoples and nations."

SUNDAY, JULY 25, 1943

An event that made a bigger impact upon white Detroit's "business
as usual" policy because it took place at the State Fair Grounds, just
north of the city, was the speech on Sunday, July 25, by Vice-President
Henry A. Wallace. He told 15,000 whites and Negroes that we "cannot
fight to crush Nazi brutality abroad and condone race riots at home."

MONDAY, JULY 26, 1943

Perhaps even more significant as omens of the immediate Detroit
future were the statements the following Monday by Wayne County
Prosecutor William E. Dowling and Detroit Police Commissioner John
H. Witherspoon. Both of these gentlemen, with Willkie's and Wallace's
warnings echoing in some of their townsmen's ears, put the responsibility for the rioting of Bloody Week squarely on the Negro community and particularly on the Negro press. The Prosecutor again
denied a petition to help create a grand jury to investigate the causes
of the riots because he had "learned" from his own investigations who
were to blame. Those to blame, he said, were a group of colored youths
who committed depredations on Belle Isle on June 20 against white
picnickers and then involved themselves in a fight on Belle Isle Bridge

as people were leaving the island. He also placed responsibility on the broadcast of a false rumor over the public-address system of a Negro night club, to the effect that a Negro woman and her child had been thrown from the bridge.

Later in the day, Prosecutor Dowling denied having said that if a grand jury came into existence "I will guarantee the NAACP [National Association for the Advancement of Colored People] will be the first to be investigated." He viewed the statements, reported the Detroit *Times*, as "ingenious fabrications" rather than as his own words. "I do charge," Dowling asserted, "and so I told the committee, that the Negro press and Martin of the Detroit *Tribune* [Louis E. Martin is Editor of the *Michigan Chronicle*, and J. Edward McCall is Editor of the Detroit *Tribune*] had fomented dissension. I do charge Martin of the *Tribune* with being the principal instigator of dissension in this area."

Accusing the N.A.A.C.P. of being a trouble-making organization, the Prosecutor stated:

They have been fomenting trouble with their crusades in the Negro neighborhoods from the start. If you want to do something constructive in this situation, you might try to control the Negro press.

The Prosecutor's accusations against the N.A.A.C.P. and the Negro press were particularly provoked, he said, by the Rev. George W. Baber, a Negro member of the Mayor's "peace board."

Rev. Baber told me [the Detroit *News* quoted Prosecutor Dowling as saying] that there were a lot of facts that he could not disclose to me, that would justify a grand jury. I asked him what these facts were. He said that he was pledged to secrecy about them, but that he had turned them over to the NAACP.

Baber's version of this event, as set forth in a sworn affidavit, is as follows:

I . . . stated that I knew persons who had information that they would present only to a Grand Jury. Mr. Dowling wanted to know what the Negroes were doing with their information. I stated that many were turning their information over to the National Association for the Advancement of Colored People to the end that proper protective measures might be pursued. Whereupon, Mr. Dowling pounded the table and jumped to his feet, saying, "Why do you turn your information over to the National Association for the Advancement of Colored People? They were the biggest instigators of the recent race riot. If a Grand Jury were called, they would be the first indicted."

Continuing in the same vein, he charged, "You people have no confidence in the law enforcement agents but turn your information over to a trouble-making organization like that."

But, as Walter White of the N.A.A.C.P. adds, in a personal statement,

Dowling . . . hastily disavowed [his extreme charge] when he found we were going to take him into court on libel.

Police Commissioner Witherspoon declared that the Prosecutor's statements conformed with the police view on the causes of the race riots. The Commissioner felt that the N.A.A.C.P. officers had been prone to listen to complaints of alleged improper conduct on the part of police officers, without attempting to investigate their correctness. "When the NAACP forwarded the unchecked claim to the department," he pointed out, "it had a tendency to encourage rather than discourage improper conduct on the part of Negroes." The Commissioner added that a study of white-Negro incidents on D.S.R. (City Department of Street Railways) vehicles in recent months showed a steady increase, with most of the trouble started by Negroes.

TUESDAY, JULY 27, 1943

The immediate effect of these charges was to re-create tension. The Rev. Horace White warned of this in a talk before the Mayor's Inter-Racial Peace Board, thus:

I went down among the Negro people after those stories came out. It was as if a bomb had been dropped. The situation is what it was just before June 21.

R. J. Thomas of the U.A.W.-C.I.O. charged that the Police Commissioner's "statements are the most serious incitement to race riots that we have had since the riots themselves." Not only did these statements arouse discussion, but they finally led Mayor Jeffries to express the conclusion that there should be a grand jury investigation, but not by a 23-man grand jury such as Councilman Edwards had proposed almost a month earlier.

THURSDAY, JULY 29, 1943

Mayor Jeffries appeared before the City Council and proposed a one-man grand jury investigation into the causes and deaths of the riots. Asserting that he believed the grand jury would not accomplish anything more than had already been done by existing investigative bodies, he added that its value would lie in the "psychological reaction" it would bring. The Mayor was supported immediately by Councilman Edwards but opposed as quickly by Council President John Lodge. The latter insisted that Council await a report on the riots which Prosecutor Dowling was preparing for submission to the Governor and which was to be made public within a few days. Councilman Comstock, in opposing the grand jury proposal, said: *"I don't like the idea of continuing this controversy by creating a grand jury to keep it alive."*

FRIDAY, JULY 30, 1943

Prosecutor Dowling revealed that four white youths were being held by the police for the confessed slaying of the aged Negro, Moses Kiska, on the evening of June 21. The four youths, all under 21, had shot Kiska while they were roaming the streets in a car "hunting niggers." Leo Tipton, Negro social director and public relations executive of the Forest Social Club, Hastings Street at Forest Avenue, was also being held. Prosecutor Dowling said that Tipton was a "key figure" in the inception of the race riots. He claimed that this publicist had grabbed the microphone at the club and had broadcast the unfounded rumor on Sunday night, June 20, that had stampeded 500 Negro patrons into wanting to "get even" with the whites.

SUNDAY, AUGUST 1, 1943

Dr. James J. McClendon, Negro physician and President of the Detroit Chapter, National Association for the Advancement of Colored People, replied in the Sunday newspapers to Prosecutor Dowling's allegations that his organization had helped to foment the race riots. As Dr. McClendon put it,

As for propaganda and the NAACP, and the local Negro press, when did it become a crime to ask that all citizens be treated fairly in a democracy? When did it become a crime to ask that loyal colored Americans be given jobs commensurate with their skill and training? . . .

No amount of NAACP militancy and propaganda could make the average Negro more mindful of discrimination and inequality than actual discrimination as practiced in the city. . . .

The founding fathers did not make their decisions on fear. Neither do we. . . .

We are fighting a war against race hatred, subjugation, and domination.

Surely all Americans ought to be willing to rid our own country of these evils. If that is propaganda, . . . we are forced to plead guilty!

Yet on that Sunday night, a number of new inter-racial incidents dangerous to racial peace took place on the cars and buses of the City Department of Street Railways. A Negro blocked a bus entrance and precipitated an altercation with the white bus driver because of the trouble the Negro was giving other passengers who wished to alight from the vehicle. As a result, the Negro struck the driver on the back of the neck with a piece of concrete. Another Negro stabbed a white streetcar conductor in the chest, arm, and back in a similar situation. Other beatings were also reported, and city officials feared another major outbreak.

                                        *   *   *   *

Over the August 1 weekend, public criticism of Prosecutor Dowling's statements issued from three distinct sources. The Executive Board of the Michigan C.I.O. Council called for a "fair, impartial grand jury investigation, under the direction of the court" and urged that Prosecutor Dowling dissociate himself from all prosecutions arising out of the race riots. The Detroit *Labor News,* organ of the Detroit and Wayne County Federation of Labor (A. F. of L.) declared that "hopes for inter-racial harmony seem to be slipping farther and farther into the background . . . with the Prosecutor and the Police Commissioner making blanket allegations that irresponsible leaders in Negro organizations were responsible for the race riot." Father Malcolm M. Dade, Rector of St. Cyprian's Episcopal Church (Negro), preached a sermon on "The Escapegoat," in which he replied to Prosecutor Dowling's accusations with the statement that the 100,000 "membership roll of the NAACP reads like a 'Who's Who' of Negro life" and that "there are very few of you [his congregation] that he doesn't include in his castigation." Since the N.A.A.C.P. also includes whites in its membership, Father Dade added that "Wendell Willkie and Col. Theodore Roosevelt are notable members of this organization."

WEDNESDAY, AUGUST 11, 1943

Governor Kelly's Fact-Finding Committee on the Detroit riots of June 20-21 made public its 8,500-word report to the Governor on August 11, nicely timed to coincide with a national convention of chiefs of police meeting in Detroit. Since this committee consisted of Wayne County Prosecutor Dowling, Detroit Police Commissioner Witherspoon, State Attorney General Herbert J. Rushton, and State Police Director Oscar C. Olander, much more than the general outlines of its report had already been set forth in previous "white papers" and other statements by the Governor, the Mayor, Dowling, and Witherspoon. This treatise—called by the press the "Dowling report"—stuck to the theory that racial tensions had been snapped "by a group of young Negro hoodlums," and it claimed that the "ordinary law enforcement and judicial agencies have thus far dealt adequately and properly with the law violators." It blamed race tensions particularly on "the positive exhortation by many Negro leaders to be 'militant' in the struggle for racial equality," and called a statement in the Detroit *Tribune* an "appeal to extract 'justice' by violence," adding:

Such appeals unfortunately have been commonplace in the Negro newspapers; can it be doubted that they played an important part in exciting the Negro people to the violence which resulted in Detroit on June 21? . . .
A theme repeatedly emphasized by these [Negro] papers is that the struggle for Negro equality at home is an integral part of the present worldwide struggle for democracy. These papers loudly proclaim that a victory over the Axis will be meaningless unless there is a corresponding overthrow in the country of the forces which these papers charge prevent true racial equality.

The report was not only singularly blind to the Federal Constitution and the Atlantic Charter; it also overlooked the responsibilities of white individuals and groups for helping to start and carry on the race riots. In this respect, Attorney General Biddle's confidential report of July 15 had been much fairer, had placed the blame on the shoulders of both whites and blacks, and had noted especially the part taken in the Belle Isle Bridge battle by white sailors from the Naval Armory.

THURSDAY, AUGUST 12, 1943

The Detroit *Free Press* quoted the Mayor as commenting, "I would say it's [the Fact-Finding Committee's] a very good report." Councilman Edwards noted pointedly that "there are still twelve unsolved murders," and he continued to demand a grand jury investigation. The *Free Press* itself called the report "wholly inadequate." Its editorial writer added, "Dowling merely shakes the tree instead of getting at the roots."

In reply to the Fact-Finding Committee's attack on the Negro press, the National Association for the Advancement of Colored People, and the Negro crime rate in Detroit, "Commentator" W. K. Kelsey replied in the Detroit *News* that in doing so the committee had "directed its main attention to three factors, none of them basic." Kelsey also pointed out that the Negro press is naturally more concerned with lynchings, race riots, and Jim-Crowism than the white publications; that the N.A.A.C.P. "is of course a thorn in the flesh of the peace authorities, as is the Civil Liberties Union and other organizations created for minority protection"; and that Negro crime cannot be understood and measured merely through reference to the number of Negroes arrested. . . .

A white religious leader observed at the same time that a "series of alleged assaults by Negroes on whites has been reported within the past week in what looks like an attempt to smear the Negroes in such a way as to prevent the thorough investigation that is being called for by all reputable groups and individuals." This minister lamented the Negro-smearing propagandas of so many city and state officials and stressed the need for making "definite changes in public attitudes and thought-life with regard to Negroes."

SUNDAY, AUGUST 15, 1943

Dr. William Allan Neilson, President-Emeritus of Smith College, and 137 other eminent Americans signed and released today an "appeal to the nation to create an atmosphere in which there can be no race riots such as that in Detroit." Here are some brief excerpts from this appeal:

Every American who loves our nation and respects the principles upon which it was founded must have been shocked and dismayed by the recent race riot in Detroit. . . .

The Detroit riot embodied many of the practices which have been associated with Nazi Germany and her partner, the Japanese Empire. . . .

In a statement on July 20, President Roosevelt declared that the recent outbreaks of violence "endanger our national unity and comfort our enemies." . . .

We call upon our people of every race, color, station and section to use all foresight in creating the atmosphere in which no battles between our people can occur.

THURSDAY, AUGUST 19, 1943

"Without even taking a formal vote," reported the Detroit *Times*, "common council today denied a new request from Mayor Jeffries for a grand jury to investigate the race riots."

Detroit's City Council thus apparently regarded the "incident" of the week of June 20 as being officially closed, except for whatever the Police Department might turn up concerning the ten or more unexplained riot deaths.

Grand jury investigations might unsettle things, and Detroit was determined to stay officially at "business as usual" as long as possible.

*   *   *   *

The race riots in Detroit were not over. They would not be over for a long time to come. Grand juries might be empaneled or be officially dismissed as legally inappropriate. New incidents in streetcars, buses, stores, and elsewhere will inevitably arise. They will make race hatreds rankle more deeply. Practice sessions with the Michigan State Troops may bring them to riot scenes in five minutes rather than the *now-scheduled* fifteen minutes. But, regardless of what additional events may occur in Detroit or in similar situations in other cities, regardless of official and popular intentions, *something much more adequate than talk must be done.* When people learn one set of lessons from their daily life-experiences, no amount of verbal propaganda or education will alter their attitudes. Something must be done in virtually every community of any size in the United States if race riots are to be minimized, if the whites and blacks are to learn how to live peaceably together in one country.

As a preparation for the construction of a program of riot prevention, as a step toward a program for the promotion of inter-racial friendship and understanding, let us analyze the Detroit race riots in terms of these questions: How were the Detroit riots handled? Who did the rioting? Who were the casualties? What really caused the Detroit riots? Did the same things happen in Los Angeles and Harlem?

Chapter 5

HOW WERE THE RIOTS HANDLED?

WALTER WHITE found "a great difference" between the Harlem riots of early August, 1943, and "the conditions in Detroit" during the week of July 20. White, Secretary of the National Association for the Advancement of Colored People, told the New York *Post* after touring Harlem in the early hours of August 2, the high point of rioting, that in Detroit "the Mayor was weak and the police inefficient. Neither condition prevails here."

How were the Detroit race riots handled? In what terms can one sum up the roles played by the Governor, Mayor, City Council, City Police, State Police and Troops, U. S. Army, citizens generally, and civic and labor organizations? Facts concerning these roles appeared throughout the chronology in Chapters 3 and 4. It will now be helpful to bring together these and other facts and also the conclusions of competent observers, to arrive at some assessment of how the race riots of Paradise Valley and Woodward Avenue were handled. In so doing, our object is not to judge individuals as such but rather to analyze techniques so that helpful lessons may be extracted from the Detroit experience and made available to the country as a whole.

To understand how the Detroit race riots were handled, it is first necessary to analyze a little more precisely how they were set in motion and how the authorities attempted to handle them at the outset. A Detroit police spokesman, as we have reported, told how "approximately 200 sailors were fighting with Negroes, and white men and Negroes were rushing into the fight," in speaking of the struggle at Belle Isle Bridge on Sunday night, June 20. A Negro co-ed of Wayne

University pointed out, "We've really had trouble ever since that Naval Armory was erected there." A news photo showed sailors, in a line from curb to curb, clearing the streets near the bridge, for traffic. A sailor on a bus the next day told one of the authors, "We fixed those black bastards last night at Belle Isle." Attorney General Biddle confirmed these statements when he said that the "prevailing hostility between sailors and Negroes inflamed the Detroit riot in its first stages."

The inference to be drawn from these points is not that the riots began necessarily as a clash between Negroes and the Navy or that a Naval unit as such assumed any responsibility in stopping the race riots. It is rather that sailors off duty have much the same prejudices and compulsions that they had under similar circumstances before they joined the Navy. Therefore, as the police spokesman stated, the sailors were fighting *against the Negroes, not* against the rioters white or black in their capacity as instruments of the law to restore peace and order. In this sense, the start of the June 20 race riots resembled the "zoot-suit" war earlier the same month in Los Angeles. There, *Time* reports that "mobs of soldiers and sailors" beat zoot-suited Mexican-Americans and left their victims to be "arrested by the Los Angeles police for 'vagrancy' and 'rioting.'" In Detroit, however, the sailors were withdrawn, and the police played a somewhat less passive role than the Los Angeles police.

The attitude of the Detroit police toward the Negroes, even when on duty, resembled that of the Los Angeles soldiers and sailors towards the Mexican-Americans. As Detroit Police Commissioner John H. Witherspoon pointed out frankly in his "white paper" of June 28,

For many years the Negroes in this and other communities have had an antagonistic attitude toward the police officer.

This feeling has been such that the policy of the department for some time has been to treat all alike, to avoid discrimination, to attempt in every manner to gain respect and to avoid at all cost any incident which might provide the spark to set off a serious race riot.

The Detroit Chapter, National Association for the Advancement of Colored People (N.A.A.C.P.), agreed with Commissioner Witherspoon's generalization in effect when it took this position, as reported in the Detroit *Tribune* of July 3:

There is overwhelming evidence that the riot could have been stopped in Detroit at its inception Sunday night had the police wanted to stop it. So inefficient is the police force and so many of its members are from the deep South, with all of their anti-Negro prejudices and Klan sympathies, that the trouble may break out again as soon as the troops leave.

This distrust of the civil authorities by Negroes even led to a "serious situation" at nearby Fort Custer Army Post when "a group of Negro soldiers in one of the quartermaster battalions . . . attempted to seize arms and trucks and start a pilgrimage to Detroit." Col. Ralph Wiltamuth, post commander said that the "men became restless over the disturbance in Detroit" and that they "wanted to go to Detroit to assist their families." He added: "Prompt action by military authorities restored order. Five men are confined in the post stockade awaiting investigation."

In other words, at the outset, the authorities of the State of Michigan and of the City of Detroit had two striking difficulties with which to cope in their efforts to restore nominal peace between whites and blacks. These difficulties were: (1) the Negroes regarded both the white sailors (although not the Federal soldiers) and the city police as anti-Negro, even as "natural enemies"; and (2) both the sailors and police demonstrated to the Negroes that they "had had enough" from the Negroes and that they would now like to "even things up."

Against this backdrop of police-Negro tension, how were the Mayor and his immediate associates equipped to handle the situation? As the attitudes and behavior of Mayor Edward J. Jeffries are summed up by an outsider, New York *PM* writer James A. Wechsler, the Mayor "wants to get a better break for minorities" but his "public record . . . is far from impressive. He has compromised, side-stepped, soft-pedalled." As Mr. Wechsler concluded, "What Detroit needs now is courageous and imaginative civic leadership." The Mayor, however, because of his indecisive role in so many race clashes, "is scorned by the 'pure whites,' distrusted by many Negroes."

The Wechsler story echoed an analysis of Detroit's race tensions made fifteen months earlier by the Federal Office of Facts and Figures, an agency later merged with the Office of War Information. The analysis was made shortly after the Sojourner Truth Homes race riots of February 28, 1942, during which the police "pointed their horses, guns, and tear gas at colored citizens" who had been accepted as tenants and were attempting to move into their new homes. "It is fairly obvious," this report indicated, "that Mayor Jeffries is not able to handle this matter constructively." It added the sharp warning that "unless some socially constructive steps are taken shortly, the tension that is developing [in 1942] is very likely to burst forth into active conflict." After fifteen more months of "nothing constructive," this prophecy's fulfilment took the form of thirty-four deaths, untold suffering, loss of morale, drop in war production, and property damage. The report also made a point of the way in which Detroit "Police seem bent on suppressing the Negroes," a situation it dwelt upon as follows:

To assume that it is necessary to suppress one side or the other to keep the peace and that the choice is to be made from the fact that the Negro group is smaller, is not only unrealistic but at this point seems to point straight to civil warfare.

With such tensions brewing, with studies being made of them by both Detroit and national agencies, one would expect the Mayor to have benefitted from such planning. He did attempt to prepare for emergencies—within the limits defined for him by his mode of operation and by the political and industrial characteristics of the "Arsenal of Democracy." The Mayor had worked out a "formula" over a period of a year for bringing in Federal troops, but it did not work. This formula required the co-operation of the Governor but did not contemplate the need for the Governor to declare martial law and to obtain a Presidential proclamation. Both these technical details of procedure, which one would have expected discussions with Army officials to have brought out long before the actual riots, apparently were unknown to Mayor Jeffries and Governor Kelly and created costly delays in obtaining Federal troops.

Mayor Jeffries summed up the control situation himself in his "white paper" of June 30 as follows:

It took us 24 hours to establish the peace after rioting broke out on the Belle Isle Bridge the night of June 20. It took us 12 hours to get the Federal troops on the scene. It took 24 hours to mobilize the Michigan troops. It took hours to clear a mob of 10,000 from Woodward Ave.
It will not take us that long next time, and again you have my guarantee on that.
The responsible authorities at all three levels of government, City, State and Federal, were greenhorns in this area of race riots, but we are greenhorns no longer. We are veterans. I admit we made some mistakes, but we will not make the same ones again.

He stressed the "tactical error" made at "about 6:30 a.m. on June 21 of thinking the race riots were under control. It was merely a lull in hostilities." He praised the rapidity with which 150 state police were rushed to the rioting scenes, adding, "If we had had 500 more of them, we would not have needed the Army." The State troops took

so long to appear because they were a recent creation, relatively untrained.

Some took the position that the chief merit of the Mayor's report
was its political technique of taking the words out of the mouths of
his opposition. He admitted and described his own errors of omission
and commission, his own indecisiveness and inadequacy. Such fairness both disarms criticism and enlists sympathy. But the Negroes had
suffered, and they were not soothed by the Mayor's explanatory techniques. Dr. James J. McClendon, President of the Detroit N.A.A.C.P.
Chapter, admitted the Mayor's inadequacies, resented the way in
which he blamed Negro distrust of police upon Negro leaders, wel-
comed his newly-appointed twelve-man Inter-Racial Committee, and
then reminded the Mayor of another such committee which he had
appointed two years before to investigate another race riot, the one
at Northwestern High School in 1941. "Today we have a new committee," Dr. McClendon said. "Its report can be written now. The
question is whether you [Mr. Mayor] will *do* anything after you
receive it."

Mayor Jeffries thus had with him at the top what he called "greenhorns." And neither he nor the "greenhorns" had put into operation
preventive measures urged by representative citizens' committees. Let
us see how well the Detroit Police Department prepared itself to
handle the race riot crisis of the week of June 20. In addition to those
already highlighted in this chapter, these qualifying factors should be
emphasized: (1) the department was 280 policemen short, owing to
war conditions; (2) the police who were to have gone off duty at midnight Sunday night remained on their posts to see the fight through;
(3) 175 police cars equipped with two-way radios enabled any
trouble area "to be reached within two or three minutes"; (4) as various reports indicate, the Negroes were antagonistic to the police,
regardless of the reasons for that situation; (5) race riots may require
special techniques with which Detroit police were not acquainted;
and (6) the police were deluged with false reports that made them
move wastefully from place to place on false alarms. This last point
made it necessary for the Police Department to utilize sixteen extra
telephone operators on Bloody Monday.

On the other hand, in opposition to such qualifying factors, the
following may also be said: (1) the police apparently regarded the
race riots until late Monday afternoon as almost wholly Negro riots
and thus permitted the gigantic Woodward Avenue mob of 10,000

whites to collect and to become menacing; (2) Philip A. Adler, columnist for the Detroit *News*, joined many citizens in wondering why
fire hoses were not used on the mobs; (3) the police exceeded their
legal prerogatives in some instances to "maintain order"; and (4) they
failed to protect Negroes.

The last three of these points require additional comment: Walter
Hardin, a Negro, International Representative of the U.A.W.-C.I.O.,
and a member of the Mayor's Bi-Racial Committee, said that a question
existed as to why the police failed to move white mobs from Woodward Avenue during the heat of the rioting when he claimed he knew
from "personal experience" how police handled such matters in industrial strikes. The following are examples of how police exceeded their
rightful duties:

1. "Police brutality which reached a new high in Negro sections of the
city during the race riot," the *Michigan Chronicle* charged on June 26,
"was felt by news photographers as well as rioters and bystanders. Langford
P. James had his arm broken by police early Monday morning while taking
a picture in downtown Detroit. A policeman struck James across the arm
with a club but did not interfere with white photographers making pictures
of the same scene. . . . Frank Brown, an official Michigan Chronicle pho-
tographer, had his camera confiscated Tuesday by police who said they
were instructed to 'take all cameras to headquarters.' The camera was later
released."

2. Social workers who were assigned to the interviewing of prisoners
reported that the police refused to permit prisoners to telephone their
families, sometimes for several days.

3. The police vilified innocent Negroes, as they did after the shooting
of Julian Witherspoon at the St. Antoine (Negro) Y.M.C.A., an incident
described in Chapter 3. The New York police during the August 2 riots
furnished a pleasant contrast to this; in many cases, they had learned to
take "Negro cussedness" smiling.

4. The police in general gave the impression of acting on the assump-
tion that a person was guilty until proved innocent.

5. Looters were in many cases apparently shot on sight. As *The Nation*
of July 3 put it, "When the white mob ran amok pulling Negroes from automobiles and streetcars, the police seem to have done little to interfere.
But when the Negroes began to retaliate on white property, the police were
quick to use both night sticks and guns." *The Nation* merely had the order
wrong; it is probable that, so far as property destruction was concerned,
the burning of cars came later after destruction and looting by Negroes.

6. On the other hand, police are also reported to have stood by and
watched looting, as if unconcerned, and with no effort in such cases to stop it.

The statement that the police did not in many cases protect Negroes is well illustrated by these quotations from eye-witnesses:

Word got around awful fast. Those police are *murderers*, [said a husky Negro of 20]. They were just waiting for a chance to get us. We didn't stand a chance. I hate 'em. Oh, God, how I hate 'em. But the fellows who had guns were ready to go. They were saying, "If it gets tight, get two whites before they get you."

Dr. B. and I were on our way to City Hall to see the Mayor [recalled a prominent white minister]. We saw a crowd leading a young colored boy up the street. It was a crowd of about 500, made up of people under 20 with the exception of an older leader. I stopped the leader and asked where he was taking the boy. Several behind him answered, "They raped our sisters; they killed the sailors." I answered, "But this little fellow didn't do anything." We finally got him to the steps of the City Hall; he was only about 13; and several policemen (who had been standing there all the time) took him into the Hall. We tried to reason with the crowd but it was impossible. I think they would have been nasty to us if we hadn't gone in.

Police "standing there all the time" frequently were merely interested spectators at Negro beatings.

In all fairness, it must be admitted with Mayor Jeffries that "the police had a tough job. A lot of them have been beaten and stoned and shot." But the difficulty of the job and the injuries suffered by individual policemen are vastly overweighed by these unassailable facts: (1) the police force and the police officials had been warned severely and over a long period of time to prepare themselves for proper action in the event of a race outbreak; and (2) the police not only failed to afford Negroes the physical protection required by law; but (3) the police actually went beyond their prerogatives at the expense of the Negroes. These three facts of police misconduct must be borne in mind by police commissioners throughout the country, if race riots are to be superseded by inter-racial peace. And another fact must be remembered with it: the notably impartial behavior of the U. S. Army troops, which commanded immediate respect from both blacks and whites. The Detroit experience proved that impartial, rather than prejudiced, policing behavior is a crucial necessity in handling a riot situation, and the Harlem experience of August 1-2, 1943, offered additional verification of this point.

The roles played by several non-governmental organizations and by the majority of Detroit citizens may be summed up briefly. The chief trade union in the area, the U.A.W.-C.I.O., immediately accepted the challenge, and its President, R. J. Thomas, passed that challenge along effectively, to the union's shop stewards and other officials—in spite of strong, known anti-Negro sentiments among the rank-and-file in certain Detroit plants. This required political bravery. In addition, the religious, civic, and labor leaders made clear their support of a decisive course of action on the parts of the Governor and the Mayor. Unfortunately this required the passage of valuable hours of time, because of the necessary arrangements that precede non-official conferences. *Effective machinery of inter-racial co-operation did not exist, after all, either in local governmental circles or unofficially.* Both the Rev. Charles A. Hill and his Citizens' Committee threw themselves with considerable speed into the work of halting the race riots. Pastor White's sound truck, and the Citizens' Committee's handbills probably helped to allay Negro fears and to speed their acceptance of an armed truce.

Chapter 6

WHO DID THE RIOTING?
WHO WERE THE
CASUALTIES?

"**I** TOOK the day off from the tool shop so I could be in the thick of it downtown," bragged the 19-year-old hoodlum later. "Jesus, but it was a show! We dragged niggers from cars, beat the hell out of them, and lit the sons of bitches' autos. I'm glad I was in it! And those black bastards damn well deserved it."

Another thrill-drunk boy of 18 boasted in much the same terms to a mature Wayne University student. This one was particularly proud to describe his personal daring when he had to crawl under a parked automobile "while a Negro three stories up in an apartment building kept shooting at the policeman standing nearby. . . . This boy," the student added, "had no reason to take part in the riots other than that the power of mob attraction just proved too much for him."

Who were the rioters? They were, to a large extent, youngsters like these, of twelve to twenty, both among the whites and the blacks; and the Detroit *News* observed that "Women participated in many of the frays with a savagery that exceeded that of men." A white woman teacher described one of the mobs across from Hudson's, the leading department store, on the afternoon of Bloody Monday in this manner:

The boys and young men in the mob were perspiring, and their eyes were bright and excited looking. Some were smoking but all were walking fast—intent on going to some destination. . . . Following this group were service men in uniform, seemingly unarmed. . . .

I thought of my own son's action when he has been excited over some out-of-the-ordinary circumstances, and I could understand somewhat how those boys felt, and I was worried—about them and for my son.

Here is a brief description of another white mob:

> By the conversation of the men gathered there [at Hamilton and Warren Avenues], I was able to detect that they were Southerners and that they resented Negroes working beside them and receiving the same amount of money. They believed that "the niggers" ought to be "taken down a peg or two."
> All of them were bare-headed, and their sleeves were rolled. They were intently discussing what they could do. More men were coming from all directions, and after I boarded the streetcar I noticed men coming through the alleys.
> Just then a car of policemen came up, and one of them called, "Break it up, boys."

But the youngsters did not furnish the deliberate leadership for the white mobs. A Negro woman described what she saw of Woodward rioting from a third-story window as follows:

> My top view, so to speak, showed clearly men in the back of the lot pushing youngsters in their teens out into the street to do the fighting, while they themselves kept back.

A Detroit *News* reporter, according to the *News* columnist Philip A. Adler, saw the same sort of thing elsewhere: "Men who led the mobs into the brawls would retreat after they had reached the fighting line, so to speak, and let others, usually boys in their 'teens, do the fighting."

An age difference was discernible among the white rioters in the two major areas of white rioting. Near the City Hall and throughout the downtown district, the bulk of the rioters were obviously in their 'teens. In the Woodward-Davenport-Mack sector, however, the most violent assaults on Negroes were perpetrated by hoodlums in their late twenties and thirties. "I recognized a lot of those fellows," said a former member of the arson squad to one of the authors. "We've had lots of trouble with them before. The whites that did most of the car burning on Woodward were from gangs of Italians, Syrians, and others who hang around bars and pool rooms, and in 'peace time' pull false alarms and that sort of thing. Almost all of them have police records. And it was the same type of Negro who did most of the fire-setting in Paradise Valley."

Other reports concerning gangs of Negro looters indicated similar youthfulness and other characteristics. A hoodlum is, after all, much the same kind of hoodlum, whether he is white or black. A Detroit *News* report told of Negro crowds in Paradise Valley in a way illustrative of this point:

As the soldiers dispersed all gatherings of young men on the street corners this morning they were met with sullen scowls but obedience. A few were jocular, these being mostly middle-aged men who shouted words to the soldiers to the effect they were glad to be able to return to work.

Such general observations contrast somewhat with the statistics on hoodlum age released by the police, but naturally police statistics are based on those who were caught and not on those who were fast enough to get away. The "Dowling Report" (issued by the Governor's Fact-Finding Committee on August 11) makes the following statements with regard to the age of the prisoners taken during the June race riots:

A fraction less than 35 percent of those detained in the rioting were 21 years of age or under.

Almost 63 percent of those detained were under 31 years of age.

Of the Negroes detained, less than 23 percent were 21 years old and under; whereas, of the whites detained, almost 48 percent . . . were 21 years old or under.

While those under 31 comprised over 66 percent of the whites detained, only a little over 60 percent of the Negroes detained were under 21 years of age.

These statistics suggest that the riotous element among the whites was younger than the same element among the colored, and that among both white and colored, it was largely the youthful, irresponsible element which participated in this tragedy.

Other details concerning arrested rioters were brought out in the report to the Governor by Dr. C. F. Ramsey of the Michigan Children's Institute. As a result of interviews by social workers, Dr. Ramsey reported on other characteristics of 310 Negroes and 30 whites. Of these prisoners, 74 percent were not recent in-migrants but had lived in Detroit for more than five years, 86 percent for more than a year; at least 45 percent were married; of those married, two-thirds had children; nearly 40 percent had high school backgrounds; and only 25 percent were roughly classified as illiterate. Thirteen percent were believed to exhibit markedly abnormal emotional tendencies.

Professors Robert L. Sutherland of the University of Texas and Julian L. Woodward of Cornell University have described the contagious emotionalism that seizes such youngsters. In their *Introductory Sociology*, they tell how the "*novelty* of the experience and the feeling of *freedom* in a crowd . . . are supplemented by . . . the tendency of repressed emotions to find expression at the first opportunity that presents itself." As they put it,

Unsatisfied prejudices, grievances, and wishes, normally held in check by the social restraints of public opinion and law, are easily released in the freedom of a crowd occasion. The more grievances and inner tensions and the less education and other inhibiting influences which one has, the more susceptible he is to the moral holiday of crowd behavior.

Or, as Dr. Arthur F. Raper says in his book on *The Tragedy of Lynching*,

Lynchings are not the work of men suddenly possessed of a strange madness; they are the logical issues of prejudice and lack of respect for law and personality, plus a sadistic desire to participate in the excitement of mob trials and the brutalities of mob torture and murder.

Few lynch-mobsters, like few Detroit race-rioters, were other than what Dr. Raper calls "unattached and irresponsible youths" of 25 and less. He adds,

Few of the lynchers were even high school graduates. . . . Most of the lynchers read but little, and were identified with but few or no organization[s].

Such generalizations should also be made concerning the black and white hoodlums of Detroit's Bloody Monday. And for much of this situation, W. K. Kelsey of the Detroit *News* blamed parents who "speak, before their children, of discrimination and hatred. The children pick up their parents' ideas without much thought or question. By the time they reach young manhood, these ideas are firmly implanted, and it requires but a spark to activate them into violence."

Some statistical characterizations of the rioters may be obtained from reports on casualties treated at City Receiving Hospital and on persons arrested. But it is well to remember that those hurt and those arrested were probably the less agile persons and, in most cases therefore, not as young on the average as those who got away. Receiving Hospital treated 433 white and Negro riot victims during the 24-hour period that ended midnight, June 21, 1943. Of these, the whites numbered 222, and the blacks, 211. Here are other figures, as reported by John F. Ballenger, Public Welfare Commissioner:

A breakdown showed 332 of the total were treated in the emergency rooms and released, of whom 185 were white and 147 were Negro. The nature of these wounds were disclosed to be: Gunshot, 12 white and 9 Negro; stabbings, 28 white and 17 Negro; beatings, 145 white and 121 Negro.

One hundred and one riot victims were hospitalized . . . of whom 37 were white and 64 were Negro. A breakdown of their injuries showed:

Gunshot, 8 white and 36 Negro; stabbings, 4 white and 7 Negro; beatings, 25 white and 21 Negro.

Seventeen . . . patients died of their injuries . . . including 3 whites and 14 Negroes. The breakdown of their injuries showed: Gunshot, 1 white and 13 Negroes; beatings, 2 whites and 1 Negro.

A breakdown of ages of the 332 who were treated and released showed that a majority of these riot victims were over 30—186 against 146 under 30. The tabulation follows:

Under 12—4; between 13 and 16—14; between 17 and 20—42; between 21 and 30—86; between 31 and 40—71; between 41 and 50—58; over 50—50. No ages were given for seven victims.

Significant aspects of this tabulation are: (1) the Negroes, although apparently better armed than white civilians, were victims of gunshot wounds inflicted by the police, in greater numbers than were whites; (2) although more whites than blacks were treated at Receiving Hospital, more Negroes were seriously injured and killed than whites, and many more Negroes probably went without hospital treatment; and (3) even though observers agreed that the mobsters were predominantly young, the victims were predominantly over 20; a majority were over 30. On the basis of the same evidence, Mayor Jeffries is quoted as reaching this different conclusion:

Receiving Hospital records show the casualties included more whites than Negroes. It is true there were more Negroes killed [25 Negroes to 9 whites, and he should have mentioned those seriously hurt], but who did the stoning?—who did the looting?—who did the shooting?

The Negroes probably held their own in the stoning and destroyed and looted more property·than did the whites, but they did not do so well in the shooting.

The report of Senior Detective Inspector Edward Graff on the 1,883 rioters arrested yields some additional information. The felony charges made against those arrested included the following: 315 "carrying concealed weapons"; 167 "breaking and entering a business place at night"; 117 looting; 28 "felonious assault"; 2 "receiving stolen property"; and 1 manslaughter; a total of 630. The misdemeanor charges ranged from 559 "disturbing the peace" to 20 "malicious destruction of property"; 10 "violating terms of the emergency proclamation" (listed by the police as "violation of martial law"); 8 assault and battery; a total of 597. Of the 656 arrested who were not charged with either felonies or misdemeanors, 617 were released by the police; the County Prosecutor's office refused to issue warrants in 27 cases; and 12 others were transferred for trial in Traffic and Ordinance

Court or for handling through the Probation Department. In addition to these 1,883 cases, the police shot 12 Negroes to death "while looting stores," and 3 other Negroes "after police were shot by them."

The question as to how much formal preparation or organization the rioters had is touched upon in some of the cases given at the beginning of this chapter; it is also treated in some detail in the next chapter under the question, What really caused the Detroit riots? At this point, it can certainly be said that older and more mature men apparently served as leaders and did not hesitate to permit their youthful following incautiously and gladly to bear the brunt of the actual fighting. A Wayne University student, too, reported that a "group at a plant where I work set aside one night a week for assaults on Hastings Street Negroes." Such a group could well provide a nucleus for one of the dangerous Woodward Avenue mobs that at one time on Bloody Monday mustered as a whole some 10,000 white men and women. Some of those who have studied Paradise Valley events contend that Negro looters gave evidence of organized tactics; trucks backed up to stores a few minutes after the rioting started and began to load merchandise brought out by the looters. Such persons as the southern real estate operator quoted in Chapter 3, as instigating confusion in the Mayor's office during Bloody Monday, and the organizations of the Ku Klux Klan type undoubtedly seized the opportunity to mobilize their weight behind what they regarded as the "just" side of the fight and a "golden opportunity"; undoubtedly there were comparable Negro elements.

From the evidence at hand, observers seem to be in general agreement that the race riots were probably spontaneous but that *the intolerant anti-Negro and anti-white forces of the community immediately and effectively canalized their support to capitalize upon the situation.*

The Casualties

In addition to considering those who did the rioting and those who paid the price in (1) death and injury, we should also recall in this connection losses in (2) morale, (3) absenteeism, (4) property, and (5) extra governmental costs. With respect to morale, it is well for us to remember that morale losses involved: (a) an intensification of the feelings of *individual insecurity,* especially as expressed in fear and distrust of Negroes by whites and of whites by Negroes; (b) the sudden growth of a kind of *social paralysis*—a tightening of the automatic controls exercised by society over its members, until these controls suppress any change whatever and all constructive social policies; (c) the *degradation of democracy as a symbol*—the loss of repute by the city in the eyes of the nation and of the nation in the eyes of a world that looks to it for democratic example and leadership; and (d) the *dangers to democracy itself* inherent in the intensification of irrational group loyalties. (These points are discussed in considerable detail in Chapter 2.)

Absenteeism, a practical consequence of the insecurity of the Negroes as well as of the holiday both white and black hoodlums enjoyed, "reduced factory operations by about 6 per cent" during Bloody Week in the Arsenal of Democracy, according to a report by William H. Hall, Manager of the Industrial Department, Detroit Board of Commerce. A spokesman for General Motors Corporation said, "Less than 40 percent of the Negroes on our seven o'clock shift [June 22, morning] reported for work." It was estimated that on that day about one-fifth of all workers were absent from their jobs, resulting in a *40-percent loss in production in the war plants.* How much this meant in terms of airplanes, tanks, and guns to be hurled against the Axis powers was not calculated. The contribution to Axis morale was greater than the loss in weapons suffered by the United Nations.

The fourth type of losses, property damages, apparently included something like $2,000,000 in merchandise looted, stores destroyed, and automobiles burned. Like Harlem in early August, "the heart of the [Detroit] Negro district had the appearance of a bombed city." Members of the Retail Grocers Association placed their loss at about $100,000. The police estimated that storekeepers received back several thousand dollars worth of loot, mostly upon information furnished by neighbors. Whether the city should bear the losses to storekeepers and possibly automobile owners became a debatable question. The Corporation Counsel of the city thought that the city should not.

Extra governmental costs, the fifth type of loss, involved many factors, far more than can be tabulated. The courts were jammed. Mayor Jeffries insisted upon the need for at least 1,000 additional city policemen. The far more successful experience of New York City in handling its Harlem riots in August has already brought realization in Detroit that police training is more important than police numbers and has led to a more adequate training program, another expense but in this case probably a cheap investment. It was estimated that the Federal troops cost the taxpayers some $100,000 a day during their occupation of the city. In addition, the Fire Department answered approximately 120 alarms on June 21, the majority for fires set by rioters. The Office of Civilian Defense, the Department of Public Welfare, and other social work agencies had to help feed the inmates of the Paradise Valley ghetto during and, for a while, after its siege.

But these property and even the immediate human losses, regardless of how large they loomed to those involved in them, were not the great considerations in discussing who did the rioting and who were the casualties. The great considerations are these: How can we diminish the number of riot-prone juveniles that we create in our industrial urban centers? How can we keep America from dividing itself more and more with walls of intolerance into increasingly warring camps—into a psychologically Balkanized country? How can we now take dramatic steps to offset the damages to American morale resulting from the anti-zoot-suit riots of Los Angeles, the Negro riots of desperation in Harlem, and the Negro-white battles of Detroit?

Who did the rioting? In many ways, this question cannot be answered through characterizing the one-thirtieth of the people of Wayne County—the Mayor said 100,000 men, women, boys, and girls, whites and blacks—who actually did the looting, stabbing, shooting, burning, beating, screaming, and running. In many ways, it can be answered only by candidly admitting that we all did the rioting, all Detroiters and all Americans. We all did the rioting in the sense that we have done little to diminish racial and religious intolerance in this country, to democratize rather than to Balkanize America's interracial and general inter-group life. We are all in the Melting Pot. The Melting Pot must be made to melt and merge its contents.

The newspapers observed that the enemies of the streets waited peaceably side-by-side in line for emergency treatment at Receiving Hospital. The Detroit *Free Press* printed a picture of dead bodies in the Wayne County Morgue with a quotation from John J. Ingalls as the caption: "*In the democracy of the dead, all men at last are equal.*"

Chapter 7

WHAT REALLY CAUSED THE DETROIT RIOTS?

R ACE RIOTS—like wars, depressions, booms—must be caused. And, in the minds of most people, they must be thought of as being caused by one man, one organization, one or at most a small number of people or things. It is difficult to face a social catastrophe and not be able to blame it on someone who can be placed in the prisoner's dock, tried by the virtuous members of society, and then "burned" in an electric chair.

That kind of explanation for human disgrace fits in with our ideas of the victory of virtue over vice, the sending of the sinner to his just rewards. That the Savior professed by most Americans came into this world "to *save* sinners" and not to pillory them escapes the reasoning of those who must have a moral and intellectual scapegoat.

The fact that the Detroit race riots were immediately blamed on almost every possible excuse at hand illustrates this common human failing. One immediately heard or read of how the mobs of whites and blacks went to war against one another because of: the weather, President Roosevelt, Mrs. Roosevelt, the Negroes, the "100% Americans," the unions, the southern whites recently arrived in Detroit, the Poles, the Jews, the Roman Catholics, Mayor Jeffries, Father Coughlin, Pastor J. Frank Norris, Gerald L. K. Smith's "America First Party," the war, strained nerves, bad housing, worse recreational facilities, and so on. Here are some sample reasonings picked up at random from the whites by a competent interviewer:

The riot was, in the last analysis, the result of efforts of the "Association for the Advancement of the Negro" [N.A.A.C.P.]. For years that organization has been working, filling the Negro with false ideas as to race equality. Many Negroes have a stereotyped reply to almost any situation—such as, "Our boys are good enough to fight for America, but not good enough for equal privileges." A small incident like the Belle Isle affair would not have had such far-reaching results had the Association not thoroughly prepared the ground in advance.

It all started long ago because the politicians have been too lenient with them. They're afraid to lose too many votes if they clamp down on them. They should have been segregated long ago. Roosevelt—Jeffries—are mostly to blame.

It looks like an organized effort because of what's been happening all over the country, New York, Los Angeles and other cities.

The colored people are mostly to blame. They can't stand prosperity.

Here are some sample Negro views:

The Ku Klux Klan started it.

Enemy agents started the whole thing.

Youngsters and 4Fs. They didn't know what mob violence was.

Nobody will ever know [why it started]. Well, some one or two people may know but they will never tell. And it doesn't matter particularly what started it. We all knew it was bound to happen.

I don't think anything that happened Sunday started it. I think it has been started from ten months ago when the migration of southern whites and illiterate Negroes started . . . and I think it was just like that in 1917 when they killed the Duke. It was just something that started it, but not that caused it.

This last explanation comes much closer than does any single cause to the explanation that facts force upon social scientists. For that matter, the Detroit race riots furnish an excellent illustration of what scientists label "multiple causes" and "multiple consequences."

Each event in our lives—marriage, war, a football game—results from a vast number of factors, persons, and events that have influenced us, the others involved in the event, and the scene of this event. And, at the same time, each human event of any importance results in a number of consequences, most of which we are not able to *predict*, many of which we are not even able to *trace*.

As the Detroit *Free Press* put it, "Detroit has been building steadily for three years toward a race riot." It might as well have said, "for a generation." As *Life* magazine summed up conclusions of *Free Press* editorialists and other writers, the following factors made large immediate contributions to Detroit Bloody Week of 1943:

(1) Detroit's abominable housing situation, which condemns thousands of white and Negro war workers to living in slums, tents and trailers;

(2) the tremendous migration of white and Negro war workers from the South since 1940; (3) "race" strikes and friction in war plants (a month ago [3,000 Packard workers walked out and 17,000 more were affected] because three Negro workers were up-graded to the assembly line); and (4) juvenile rowdyism, which has increased during the war (last month 100 white and Negro youths fought a pitched battle in a Detroit playground).

To this, *Life* added these longer term aspects:

Although the riot was definitely a victory for Adolf Hitler and other enemies of the U. S., there was no evidence that it had been planned by foreign agents, local Fascists or anyone else. It broke out suddenly on a hot Sunday night, and its basic cause was an old, ugly fact in U. S. life: prejudice and misunderstanding between the white and black races.

Let us elaborate this estimate with the aid of some facts and illustrations concerning (1) the Red Cross and the armed forces, (2) in-migration and employment, (3) overcrowding in dwellings, recreation, transportation, (4) delinquency and crime, and (5) prejudiced attitudes.

1. *The Red Cross and the Armed Forces*

The Negro race has resented deeply that the blood it has given to Red Cross "blood banks" is segregated from "white blood." Even though physicians, physiologists, and physical anthropologists have assured the Red Cross that the blood plasma of the two races is chemically indistinguishable and may be used interchangeably without any possible damage to patients, the Red Cross has continued to Jim-Crow Negro blood plasma, and Negroes throughout the country have continued to tear up Red Cross pledge cards. Negroes say: "They are treating our blood as though we are not human." "This is one of the greatest insults of all."

In addition to this provocative policy, the newspapers—both white and Negro—have carried accounts of Negro-white clashes in Army camps, the segregation of Negro soldiers in Negro units and in Jim-Crow transportation facilities, and the traditional limitation of Negroes to few jobs other than mess attendants in the Navy. The Negroes are supplying their share of soldiers, and, as the National Urban League (Negro-white) has put it in a pamphlet on *The Negro and National Defense,* "there must be no question as to the Negro's loyalty and willingness to defend his country." But many Negroes still tell public opinion interviewers:

Our boys in camps [are] being treated so bad.
They make Jim Crow of the soldiers.

They're just not being given a fair chance [in the Army].
They're putting up their lives for nothing to fight for.

These statements remind one of the charge by Judge William H.
Hastie when he resigned in 1943 as civilian aide to Secretary of War
Stimson. Hastie, a Negro who was concerned with the morale of Negro
soldiers, said that the War Department has "an anti-Negro bias that
made [his] work there a travesty." Opinion pollers also found that,
among the Negroes,

One-half feel the *Air Force* is all but closed to them.
One out of three is pessimistic about the *Navy*.
Three in ten feel Negroes have little chance of becoming *officers*.
Only one in ten is similarly discouraged about Negro chances in the
WACS.

And the Detroit Negroes were found by these reporters to be "con-
sistently more skeptical of colored people's chances in the armed
forces" than Negroes elsewhere.

These Red Cross and armed-forces situations are parts of the
Detroit picture that must be remembered in thinking of the causes of
the 1943 race riots.

2. *In-Migration and Employment*

"Commentator" W. K. Kelsey analyzed the riots in the Detroit
News the day after Bloody Monday, as follows:

The present fracas is due to the fact that the immensity of the war
work here has brought scores of thousands of people to Detroit who have
encountered new conditions to which they apply old standards. Southern
whites have come here in vast numbers, bringing with them their Jim
Crow notions of the Negro. Southern Negroes have come here to take
jobs which give them for the first time in the lives of many of them a
decent wage, and a sense of freedom they have never known before. Some
of them have become, in white opinion, too "uppity." The embers smoldered
a long time, and at last a slight incident caused them to burst into flame.

The effort to make Detroit conform to Kentucky "hillbilly" and Georgia "red neck" notions of white domination is reflected in frequent
white comments in buses and streetcars and bars, such as: "It wouldn't
have happened down home. We know how to keep niggers in their
place." "Southern niggers aren't like these bold brassy Northern
niggers." As a comment, too, on the headline, "20 NEGROES KILLED
IN RACE RIOT," some whites commented, "Served them right. They
were getting too chesty anyway."

The statistical picture beneath these patterns makes them clearer: In 1916, Detroit had about 10,000 Negroes; in 1925, about 80,000; in 1940, about 160,000; in 1943, about 220,000. During the past three years, the entire population of Detroit had increased from 1,600,000 to roughly 2,100,000 or more. The 440,000 whites added during these three years came from Canada, the Middle West, the East, but by all odds the most riotous potentially came chiefly from the South: Kentucky, Tennessee, Oklahoma, Arkansas. They, like the Negroes, were refugees from the sharecropper system of Negro-white peonage, from blighted land and stunted opportunities. As Isaac Franck, a social work executive, has analyzed the situation:

> There has been a large influx of southern white[s]. . . . They are ignorant and hold traditional southern attitudes toward the Negroes. Socially, they are classed with the "foreign" elements in Detroit. They are in great need for compensation—to look down upon other groups. The Negroes make a convenient target. . . . [The southern whites] have moved into the best areas and have no basic community ties. They constitute a thoroughly dislocated element in the population.

Even though in March, 1943, Negroes constituted roughly 10 percent of Detroit's population, their industrial gains had only given them 8.4 percent of the jobs and those the poorer ones in 185 major war plants in the Detroit area; 55 of these plants employed less than 1 percent Negroes. Of the 107,000 women employed in these same plants at that time, less than 3,500 were Negroes, and these few were holding largely custodial positions. Walter White of the N.A.A.C.P. also makes the statement,

> It is significant that so far as I know not one important industrialist or employer or employers' association in Detroit has taken any public position on the riot. On the contrary, as in the Packard strike, some of the officials of companies have definitely encouraged rioting against Negroes.

3. *Overcrowding in Dwellings, Recreation, and Transportation*

Add 60,000 new in-migrants to slum areas in which few of 160,000 Negroes living there previously had had more than the most abject slum conditions. To this add the fact that all the Negroes began making more money than they had had since the 1920's and much more than the new Negro in-migrants had ever had. And then you have the beginnings of a conception of the internal pressures that developed in Detroit's Negro ghettos, especially the one surrounding Paradise Valley. The Negro population was literally "bursting out of its seams." Take an already crowded situation, add half again as many people, give them a great purchasing power, and still attempt to confine them within approximately the old area, and the pressures developed within that increasingly inadequate "container" will burst the walls.

The Detroit *Tribune* (Negro) summed up the situation on July 3, 1943, thus: "During this same period when living standards were gradually rising and Negroes had a little more money to improve their conditions, they were nevertheless forced to remain in restricted areas, huddled together in shelters with leaky roofs, crumbling interiors, unsafe stairways and bad plumbing." Beneath a photograph of such an interior, the *Tribune* commented:

The dwelling . . . is typical. . . . The unsanitary edifice, which was formerly used for a church, housed 18 Negro families, most of the groups occupying one room [each]. Here the couple, their girls and boys must eat, sleep, play, work, seek a new start each morning and comfort each night.

Some 3,500 houses in the Paradise Valley district have only outside toilets in shacks over holes in city sewer mains to provide "sanitary" facilities. A city housing expert points out that any improvement in the slum dwellings short of rebuilding would merely make it all the more difficult to put through slum clearance projects "some day." The *Seventh Annual Report* of the Detroit Housing Commission (covering chiefly 1941) states that "50.2 per cent of all dwellings occupied by Negroes were found to be substandard, while only 14 per cent of the white dwellings were substandard."

This housing situation had one of its crises in the Sojourner Truth Homes race riots of February 28, 1942. The *Tribune* described this event as follows:

On the day that Negroes, who had been accepted as tenants in the project, attempted to move in, hundreds of whites blocked the roads, stoned cars and trucks and brutally beat unsuspecting Negroes. As is shown above [in an accompanying picture], police pointed their horses, guns and tear gas at colored citizens who grouped themselves for protection and allowed the whites to congregate and openly display weapons.

At that time, Negroes and their white sympathizers used as a slogan "WE WANT HOMES NOT RIOTS." They got a few more homes but chiefly they got the riots.

From the standpoint of the relations of the dwellers in the Negro slums with those in the nearby white slums, one's attention is immediately focused upon two dramatically opposing processes: (1) a tremendous accumulation of pressures within the hemmed-in Negro district, expressed in terms of high rents, bad facilities, and insolent landlords; (2) sharp defensive movements by landlords, real estate interests, and "unmixed" white slum dwellers to keep the Negro community from expanding in directions where the landlords and real estate interests fear that Negro occupancy would lower property values.

Recreation facilities in both the white and the black slums match the dwellings in inadequacy. "The kids particularly," said a Detroit newspaperman, "get tired of the bars and juke joints. You go in those places any night and you see them sitting around with perfectly vacant faces. They don't know what to do with themselves. They don't even talk. . . . Aren't they ready for any kind of excitement?" Few playgrounds, almost no swimming pools, the newspaperman's picture is an accurate one. No wonder that Msgr. Francis J. Haas, Chairman of the Federal Fair Employment Practice Committee, stressed "inadequate housing, recreation and public transportation" in discussing factors responsible for the 1943 race riots.

A person said to be a "high official in Detroit's housing projects" is quoted by Philip A. Adler in the Detroit News as calling the Negro housing situation "appalling."

Even in normal times, rent in the Negro slums was about two or three times higher than in white districts [he said]. A hovel, worth about $10 a month, rented in the Negro section for about $25. A five-room shack, which would normally rent for about $25 a month, often is rented out to five families, one room to a family, at $10 to $15 per month each.

With housing preference given in the war industries to in-migrant Negroes, the old Negro families in Detroit, even those engaged in war production, have been left with no place to go, even at the exorbitant rents they are paying. Detroit's Negro housing is one of the sorest spots in our economy.

It is little wonder, therefore, that the Negro 10 percent of Detroit is said by Adler to contribute 65 percent of the people the police arrest, called by some 65 percent of the "community's crimes."

4. Delinquency and Crime

The imprisoning walls of the slums breed frustrations, and these frustrations of overcrowding demand outlets that take the forms of juvenile delinquency and crime as well as diseases and other symptoms of moral and social disintegration. And these social and physical diseases do not confine themselves to their breeding grounds but spread their venoms over the rest of the community. The Negro aspect of overcrowding, delinquency, and crime is summed up by Adler thus:

Trouble began with the growth of the Negro community after the [first world] war. To the police this meant that the Negro settlement had become a hotbed of blind pigs, brothels and gambling joints. It was then that the KKK began to grumble about sending Negroes back "where they belonged."

Social workers knew better. They knew the Negroes belonged where they were, since the Detroit industries needed them for the menial jobs which the white men would not do. As for immorality, this, to the social workers, white as well as black, meant simply that the Negroes' social and cultural level was not rising as fast as their financial and economic status. The solution was more education.

During the war days, both before and after Pearl Harbor, juvenile delinquency in particular was vastly on the increase among both whites and Negroes. It could be said of Detroit as J. Edgar Hoover, F.B.I. Chief, said of the nation, that the "arrests of 'teen age boys and girls, all over the country, are staggering. Some of the crimes youngsters are committing are almost unspeakable. Prostitution, murder, rape. These are ugly words. But it is an ugly situation." Little wonder that he said, "This country is in deadly peril. We can win this war, and still lose freedom for America. For a creeping rot of moral disintegration is eating into our nation." The same could be said and was said of the under-war-age youth of Detroit, the youngsters who were numbered among the 100,000 race rioters of Paradise Valley and Woodward Avenue.

5. Prejudiced Attitudes

Student interviewers found relatively few "impartial" observers of the Detroit race riots, and those few they found were mostly fellow students and their teachers. Interviews with 166 mixed Detroiters on Bloody Monday indicated this rough line-up of sentiments: strongly pro-white, 53%; pro-white, 17%; impartial, 17%; pro-Negro, 10%; and strongly pro-Negro, 3%. A more general poll, more systematically undertaken, would have revealed an even greater polarization of Detroit sentiments, in the estimation of the interviewers and of the authors. The race riots, at least temporarily, drove the races farther apart than before, into two suspicious and fearful "camps."

But these prejudices were not created by the race riots. They were merely rendered more vocal, more sharply defined. Such conversations as the following were overheard:

Such brutality and lawlessness should be stopped! It's horrible the way they have beaten the Negroes.

But, Carrie, they're only *niggers*, and everyone knows that niggers *always* revert to that cannibal blood in them and *always* kill or something!

Such myths are of long standing, like the elements out of which developed these remarks:

Do you know what is going to happen next? There's going to be a battle between Jews and niggers, and the Governor's bringing in 15,000 troops.

And this report by a Wayne University student bears out the same point:

I talked to many who were usually decent, respectable people who thought the treatment of Negroes was all right. A reason given for the approval was that the colored people had killed several people and looted white stores. . . . Incidentally, these same people are also prejudiced against Jews but still they said they were in sympathy with the Jews whose stores were looted.

On the Negro side, the stimulation of intolerance is illustrated by this report by another student:

A colored woman who had worked for years in this home and had become a part of the family, appeared for work the day of the riot. Things went along as usual that day, but the following morning Rosa appeared late and with disheveled hair and demanded her pay. "I ain't goin' ta work for white trash no more," she asserted. "You'll be workin' for *me* soon instead!"

The sources of anti-Negro, anti-White, and similar prejudice are not in the schools, the churches, and like organizations. Sentiments of prejudice begin in the intimate social relationships of home and play-group, and they develop and solidify into deepset habit patterns chiefly through ignorance—ignorant mothers and fathers who try to give their children a feeling of status through "running down" other groups and races—ignorant associates in play and work activities. *All this is ignorance that we have failed to dispel through positive preparations for democratic living.* These prejudices provide emotional satisfactions, which are then fanned by irritations of all kinds, by demagogic orators, by organizations that feed upon hate, and by such subversive groups as the Christian Front, the Black Legion, the Ku

Klux Klan, and the many others that proselytize the psychologically conditioned with wonderfully satisfying "panaceas."

From the other side of the picture—the positive examples, in Detroit and other places—we are able to see what the curative answer is, at least in part and on a short-term basis. When Rev. Gerald L. K. Smith's followers picketed Wayne University because a Negro poet was scheduled to address an assembly, the students argued with the pickets, tried to make the pickets understand the injustice of their attitude. And the students turned out in a body to hear the poet Langston Hughes. In much the same way, other Detroit experiences indicate that Negroes and whites who have been prepared for working together and who have worked together in the same plant long enough to become "neighborly," do not fight against each other when a race riot breaks out. Similarly, Negroes and whites who have lived in mixed areas long enough to have become adjusted to each other's presence and characteristics, see no reason to riot against each other.

The answer to prejudice in action—the answer to this general *psychological condition* fundamental to race friction—consists, therefore, in persistent realistic education along the lines of inter-racial co-operation. This is not the whole answer or the only answer, and it does not cope with basic causes. But it is a positive and practicable method of coping with inter-racial frictions in the present period. Many elements today contribute toward racial intolerance and other group intolerances, making them probably worse than they have ever been before in our country. Such constructive procedures as are suggested in the third section of this book now become imperative.

Chapter 8

DID THE SAME THINGS HAPPEN IN LOS ANGELES AND HARLEM?
THE RIOT PATTERN

" **A** WHITE cop shot a Negro soldier."
"Them cops got it coming to them."
As New York's *PM* pointed out editorially after the Harlem Negro riots of August 1 and 2, 1943, "these two statements . . . link Harlem and Detroit, Harlem and Beaumont, Harlem and Mobile, Harlem and Los Angeles. It is not a question as to whether the statements are true or false. What is important is that they epitomize what Negroes are feeling, not only in New York, but everywhere throughout the country."

The Harlem riots differed, however, in at least three marked respects from those in June in Detroit. In the first place, the Negroes in Harlem did not clash with white gangs; they rioted out of sheer frustration, the frustration of black men in a white man's world. They looted, destroyed property, and badgered the police out of sheer desperation or "cussedness" at being outcasts, members of a degraded caste, in the only country they know and love, *a country in which they have lived for a greater average period of time than their white neighbors.* In the second place, the way in which the Mayor and the police handled the Harlem Negro riots was much different from that of Detroit. In New York, the "police have acted most admirably," said New York City's Negro Councilman Adam Clayton Powell. "They have proved themselves New York's finest." No outstanding Detroit Negro made such a statement concerning Detroit's police. And a third highly significant difference between the situations in Harlem and in Paradise Valley is that no notable "climate of intolerance" existed among the whites in New York; New York in August, 1943,

98

had no counterparts of Father Coughlin, Gerald L. K. Smith, Pastor
J. Frank Norris.

The *incident* that set off the Harlem riots of 1943 did not seem
sufficiently serious to inspire violence to kill 5; injure at least 307
(including 53 policemen) and possibly 600; destroy some $5,000,000
worth of property, chiefly grocery stores and pawn shops; and occasion the arrest of 450. An Assistant District Attorney described the
incident as follows:

> Pvt. Robert Bandy, a [Negro] military policeman, . . . was in the lobby
> of the Hotel Braddock . . . with his mother, checking out. He noticed that
> two women and three men who had rented a room were requesting their
> money back. The room clerk refunded all of the money except one dollar.
> They were asked to wait at the desk until the elevator operator came down-
> stairs before they were to get the rest of their money.
> Margie Polite, 33, one of the . . . women . . . became very disorderly.
> [Patrolman James] Collins was called to the desk by the clerk to keep order.
> Bandy noticed the officer pushing Miss Polite out and became involved.
> He remarked to the policeman: "You wouldn't do that to one of your
> group."
> The two became involved in a fight. Collins threw his nightstick at
> Bandy and missed, according to Bandy's mother and sweetheart. Bandy's
> mother entered into the brawl. Bandy picked the nightstick up. Collins
> ordered him to put it down and then fired a shot. It struck Bandy in the
> upper part of his shoulder. It was not a serious wound.
> Angry crowds gathered around and attacked the patrolman again,
> according to Bandy's mother and sweetheart. Rumors spread quickly that
> a Negro soldier had been killed by a policeman in the Braddock lobby.
> That was the beginning.

This event was similar to the one that set off Harlem's previous riots
of March 19, 1935. On that day a 16-year-old Negro boy had been
caught after stealing a pen-knife. Growing hysterical, he bit the hand
of his captor. The arrival of an ambulance to treat the captor's hand
set off the rumor that a Negro boy had been "badly beaten." That
rumor collected crowds and precipitated damaging riots.

In the 1943 Harlem outbreak, not only did city officials take decisive
and immediate action, but civic and labor bodies also moved effectively
and rapidly. Within two hours of the outbreak of violence late Sunday
night, August 1, many white and Negro C.I.O. officials were touring
"the streets of Harlem urging its residents to remain peaceful and
return to their homes," reported Saul Mills, Secretary-Treasurer of the
Greater New York Industrial Union Council, and he added, "Many instances occurred throughout Sunday night and Monday where mobs

on the Harlem streets booed and refused to listen to city and other officials in their appeals for order but were receptive to appeals from C.I.O. and other labor representatives." The following day, City Councilman Powell called a special meeting in his Abyssinian Baptist Church which brought together more than 250 Negro, labor, civic, and church officials. This representative group drafted a citizens' emergency program and sent it to the Mayor in the hands of a special committee.

Particularly significant in the 1943 Harlem riots was the decisive manner in which Mayor F. H. LaGuardia *immediately* (1) took control of the situation, (2) utilized as many Negro policemen, military police, and air raid wardens as he could make available, (3) quarantined the area of the disorders and sizable adjoining areas, (4) concentrated sufficient police power in every dangerous block to halt looting, rioting, and other hoodlumism without further ado, and (5) persisted in his efforts until all symptoms of disorder had abated. The intelligence with which Negroes were utilized to control the situation is suggested by the fact that the 125th Street Precinct issued nightsticks to 300 Negro civilians, many of them volunteers requested from trade unions; they were given OCD (Office of Civilian Defense) armbands and told by the police to stand by for duty. It was generally agreed that the riot had stemmed from essentially the same mounting tensions and dissatisfactions that had brought bloodshed and property destruction elsewhere, especially those directed against the police as available symbols of white control and against grocers and pawnshop-operators as available symbols of white exploitation. As Roi Ottley puts it in his book, *New World A-Coming* (1943), in Harlem "food prices are considerably higher than in other parts of the city. For every dollar spent on food, the Negro housewife has to spend at least six cents in excess of what the housewife in any other comparable section is required to pay."

Of the many specific irritants that had brought about the "Negro Uprising" in Harlem on August 1, the segregation of Negro men and women in the armed services was stressed most frequently and urgently by investigators. Such, for example, was the judgment of Walter White, Secretary, National Association for the Advancement of Colored People, and of Joseph Kelly of the Industrial Union of Marine & Shipbuilding Workers, Chairman, New York C.I.O. Committee for the Abolition of Racial Discrimination. Other "basic causes" listed by Kelly were:

2. The failure of the OPA [Office of Price Administration] to enforce ceiling prices and to establish strict control over rents.

3. Failure of the Congress and the OPA to roll back food prices to the level of September 15, 1942.

4. Failure of the FEPC [Federal Fair Employment Practice Committee] to carry out its original program of full investigation of discriminatory hiring practices with prosecution of firms guilty of violating the President's Executive Order barring job discrimination on grounds of race, color or creed.

5. Failure of the Congress to pass the anti-poll tax bill.

6. Failure of the [New York] State Committee on Discrimination in Employment to investigate and to enforce violations of the State Civil Rights Law.

7. Failure of Governor Dewey and the State Legislature to appropriate funds authorized by the Constitutional Amendment of 1938 for the construction of new housing.

8. Lack of adequate housing, health, hospital, school, playground and recreational facilities due to the pinch-penny attitude of the Mayor, the Board of Estimate and the City Council.

9. Failure of the Mayor and the City government to follow up the constructive suggestions contained in the report of the Mayor's Committee on Harlem submitted to the Mayor in 1935.

10. Failure of city officials, following the race riots in Detroit, Beaumont, Los Angeles, etc., to set up a broad and representative citizens' committee on inter-racial cooperation to make specific and constructive plans for the alleviation of the social and economic conditions affecting the Negro population and for the continual improvement of inter-racial friendship.

The Los Angeles riots differed in significant ways from those in Harlem and Detroit. First, the Los Angeles riots can properly be called a "zoot-suit race war," because they persisted over a greater number of days than the Detroit or Harlem riots even though the deaths, injuries, and property damage were less. They also differed in these respects: In Los Angeles, gangs of soldiers and sailors did the fighting against zoot-suited *pachucos*, little Mexican-American youths. *Time* quoted a 12-year-old zooter with a broken jaw as saying, "So our guys wear tight bottoms on their pants and those bums wear wide bottoms. Who the hell they fighting, Japs or us?" When the soldiers and sailors had dragged a zooter from a theater and beaten him to the ground, the police moved in and arrested—the zooter . . . for "vagrancy" or "rioting." In Los Angeles, too, the Hearst *Examiner* and *Herald & Express* and the Chandler *Times* did not take the constructive stand observed in the Detroit and the New York newspapers. On the contrary, late afternoon editions signaled the worst outbreak with what *Time* calls "a purported anonymous call to headquarters: 'We're meeting 500 strong tonight and we're going to kill every cop

we see.' The Hearst *Herald & Express* bannered: ZOOTERS
THREATEN L. A. POLICE." "Panzer" divisions of soldiers and sailors
provided the police with plenty of Mexican-American zoot-suited
youths to arrest that night.

Rather than from an incident that permitted seething tensions to
roar forth into destructive action, the Los Angeles race riots developed
by stages out of a pattern of revolt against the impervious "white
front," a pattern into which the second-generation Mexican-Americans
had gravitated. As *Time* analyzes it,

> Their fathers and mothers were still Mexicans at heart. They themselves
> were Americans—resented and looked down on by other Americans. Job-
> less, misunderstood in their own homes and unwelcomed outside them,
> they had fallen into the companionship of misery. They dressed alike, in
> the most exaggerated and outlandish costume they could afford: knee-length
> coats, peg-top trousers, yard-long watch chains, "ducktail" haircuts.

And they not only made themselves obvious by their dress; they
also marked themselves out for persecution by taking to running in
gangs and making raids on parties. They even made the mistake of
using their knives on some isolated sailors on dark streets. As a result,
to quote again *Time's* careful account in its June 21, 1943, number,

> If the *pachucos* had asked for trouble, they got more than was coming
> to them last week. The military authorities were notably lax (all shore and
> camp leave could easily have been canceled), the Los Angeles police
> apparently looked the other way. The press, with the exception of the
> *Daily News* and Hollywood *Citizen-News*, helped whip up the mob spirit.
> And Los Angeles, apparently unaware that it was spawning the ugliest
> brand of mob action since the coolie race riots of the 1870's, gave its
> tacit approval.

Despite the differences between these riots and those in Detroit,
certain significant similarities emerge from these and other riots studied.
And these similarities point to the fact that a "pattern" of race riots
exists that can be generalized in the form of a series of probable steps.
This pattern is helpful both as a means of understanding the nature
of race riots and also as an aid in predicting areas in which they are
likely to occur.

The Riot Pattern

Granted conditions that make the whites and blacks in an area
prone to riot (such as are summed up in Chapter 7 and generalized in
Chapter 9), race riots *may* involve the following steps:

1. *An event*, usually after a series of irritating events that dramatized

race frictions upon a rising crescendo. The climactic event may not be any more dramatic than many that preceded it, but it has to lead to the next two steps if a race riot is to result.

2. *A crowd gathers.* This focuses attention upon the event and furnishes the media through which hysterical, inciting rumors travel.

3. *Milling,* like a herd about to stampede. The mob moves around, taking some part in the climactic event (as in Detroit and Harlem), starting the riots immediately.

4. *Communication of excitement.* Through the milling process the crowd excites itself more and more, and individuals break off to warn friends, get recruits, pass on rumors and hysterical excitement.

5. *Loss of critical self-consciousness.* Mob anonymity absolves the individual of responsibility for destructive acts. This is exhibited in bragging statements from the mouths of rioters.

6. *Brutalized emotions rise and are given sanction by the mob.* This phenomenon is discussed in detail in the next chapter in connection with the analysis of two-sided or ambivalent sentiments and their relation to opinions.

7. *Leadership* from the most excited and violent or from the most clear-eyed and depraved.

8. *Movement to new actions* against the objects chosen for violence, members of the other race or possessions or even symbols of the race, such as policemen, grocery stores, and pawnshops.

From a roof top, all of this looks as though the mob is rapidly going "out of its mind." And the generation of such mass hysteria shows the character of insanity, except that the members of the mob are not nearly as uncontrolled, impulsive, and depraved alone as they become under mob-suggestion. In the race-riot mob, no rules apply, no fair play. No ethics of any kind have meaning except the crude ones of the human-pack, even more brutal than the wolf-pack.

Within the race riot mob, the following degrees of participation may be noted: (1) young leaders (the most excited and violent mobsters, the ones whom the rank-and-file emulate); (2) older leaders (vicious middle-aged hoodlums or natural leaders who believe that the incident beginning the riot endangers "their people," "their homes," "their safety"); (3) rank-and-file rioters, who participate but not on the fervid scale of the young leaders; and (4) bystanders, who enjoy vicariously but emphatically the emotional "jag" of being a part of the "show" without taking the risk of doing any of the fighting or other activity. The spirit of the latter reminded one of the authors of the way in which Chicago bystanders paid for pieces of blotting paper that had allegedly been dipped in the blood of a gangster a few minutes after officers killed him in front of a downtown theater crowd.

The aftermath of a riot has these chief characteristics: (1) pride of accomplishment on the part of participants of both racial groups regardless of the outcome; (2) an absence of guilt feelings, justified by the fact that so many were associated with them in the riots and that they had such "excellent" and "moral" reasons for their actions; and (3) a stimulation of organization to prepare for the "next time," based upon the *esprit de corps* created by common experience and alleged threats to the welfare of the social group or race represented. These naturally are characteristics, we want to insist, of the rioters and vicarious rioters, not of the population in general.

In short, the riot pattern cannot be eliminated by suppression alone. On the contrary, suppression may merely "sweep" surface symptoms "under the carpet" and force the riot-prone to organize more thoroughly for their next outbreak. What is needed is an intelligent diagnosis of this social disease and then an adequate course of treatment. In other words, we must have a program for riot prevention that will attack the causes of riots in a broad and adequate fashion. Efforts to systematize such diagnosis and treatment are made in Part III of this book.

III. WHAT MUST AMERICA DO?
A Program for Preventing Race Riots

IF THESE SYMPTOMS APPEAR...

"UNLESS some socially constructive steps are taken shortly, the tension that is developing is very likely to burst into active conflict."

"Two months ago everybody in Detroit familiar with the situation knew that race riots were inevitable."

The first of these sentences was written *fifteen months before* the Detroit race riots of the Bloody Week in 1943. It is from a confidential report of the Federal Office of Facts and Figures—finally released in the newspapers on June 28, 1943—a report that was made just after the February 1942 riots at the Detroit Sojourner Truth Federal Housing Project. The second sentence is from the Detroit *Free Press* of June 22, 1943, the morning after Bloody Monday.

Publications of the trade unions and of Negroes were also pointing to the menacing situation. The *Wage Earner*, a labor organ, early in June urged Detroit to recognize "the ugly truth that there is a growing, subterranean race war going on in the city of Detroit which can have no other ultimate result than an explosion of violence, unless something is done to stop it." The June *Racial Digest* carried an article, "Detroit Is Still Dynamite," and the May, 1942, (*sic*) number of the Negro magazine, *Opportunity*, described the "feel" of Detroit thus: "There is something ominous like the low rumble of distant thunder before a storm."

In short, the riots came to Detroit as a shock but not as a surprise. But how was it possible that so many people knew that the Detroit race riots were coming? What were the storm signals? How can a community tell when inter-racial tensions are nearing the breaking point? What is the breaking point?

The first step in the prevention of race riots is to learn to spot symptoms, to develop foresight. Hindsight is easy enough. Post-riot investigations can reveal causes, but such exercises must not stop with the mere satisfaction of curiosity. Such investigations, to be useful, must yield a knowledge of diagnosis that will enable us to distinguish fever symptoms before the crisis appears. Our contention is that, even as an early cancer can be cured when discovered, racial explosions can also be prevented when their causes are attacked in time.

There are eight areas in which to look especially for the symptoms of the riot virus:

1. Opinions and sentiments
2. Rumors—the verbal "milling process"
3. Racial frictions
4. Demagogic groups
5. Juvenile delinquency
6. Police behavior
7. Overcrowding
8. Employment.

Some examples and pointers will indicate more clearly the kinds of symptoms that appear in these areas.

1. Opinions and Sentiments

Opinions are what we *say* we think about things, events, persons, or whatever. But sentiments are our deep and emotional likes, dislikes, and drives to action. We can easily report our opinions, but our sentiments lie largely in subconscious areas of our minds. It is difficult for us to distinguish our own sentiments. It is consequently much more difficult to distinguish the sentiments of other individuals and other groups.

Opinion is always a "surface reaction" to ideas and issues of a public sort that are being discussed. In other words, it is what a person willingly tells a relatively unknown interviewer. Opinion is thus conscious, verbal, sometimes falsified to conform to "the right thing to say," inconstant, not too difficult to change within the limits set by people's sentiments, and rather easily measured.

Sentiment, on the other hand, is more emotional, less organized, and more stable. In other words, it is what "we really *feel*" towards another person, group, idea, or issue. People thus do not like to reveal their sentiments and, to a marked extent, do not actually put them into words or even understand the nature of these "main springs" of their thought and action. Psychiatrists have discovered that people's sentiments are often contradictory and that they really change very slowly and are difficult to ferret out and measure.*

The distinction between opinions and sentiments is especially significant in the race-tensions field, since opinions do not always reveal the tenseness of the brewing strife. It is also necessary as preparation for the complicating fact that sentiments are frequently "two-faced," or, as the psychiatrists say, "ambivalent." Psychiatrists know that our sentiments towards others frequently contain both affection and hate, tolerance and detestation. When conditions are favorable, we treat a given person decently or even fondly. At other times, upon relatively slight provocation, blind fury may flare up between us.

What are some of the symptoms of riots-in-the-making that you are likely to find? Is it enough to be skeptical of first impressions and to look for the ways in which Negroes and whites "really think about each other"? The points to remember are:

1. We must first get as intimate a picture as possible of Negro and white *sentiments* in the community in question.

2. We must watch carefully for evidences of a shift in race opinions caused by a shift in the underlying two-sided sentiments. As in personal relations, that shift may occur with what looks like relatively slight provocation, and such shifts from reasonable tolerance to blind riotous hate may begin to sweep our community. A sudden upsurge in open statements against the other race is a definite symptom of this emotional shift, a symptom that immediately precedes a riot, but *it is a shift we can predict if we understand Negro and white sentiments.*

So much for opinions and sentiments themselves. Let us survey briefly the kind of symptoms one finds among rumors and racial frictions, two areas of activity that powerfully influence both opinions and sentiments.

---

* This distinction between opinions and sentiments was described by Alfred McClung Lee and Willard Waller in a paper delivered in 1942 before the National Association of Public Relations Counsels.

2. Rumors—the Verbal Milling Process

As people "mill around" in their ordinary day-to-day lives, rumors are common enough, rumors about all sorts of things. These rumors are largely random and seldom important beyond the individuals involved. But as racial tensions mount, the rumors that circulate take on a nastier and more purposive character. They cease being merely idle gossip with little or no basis in fact and become more biting and direct in their dynamic contributions to the more and more rapidly turning whirlpool of mob hysteria.

Rumors symptomatic of race riots generally go through three chief stages:

1. They begin with tales of alleged insults and discriminations, frequently traceable to subversive groups.

2. Then come stories of imminent violence, of arming by the other race, of the need to protect one's home and loved ones, of invasion from another city.

3. Finally one hears the crisis rumors, the inflammatory accounts of sex assaults, beatings, and murders.

In riots as in most human activities, particularly those of a criminal nature, the participants exhibit a striking anxiety to obtain "moral justification" for their actions. Lynchers thus pride themselves on protecting their "women folks," even though any sober student of society recognizes the threat to all human rights inherent in lynch-mob tactics. Even thieves and murderers and prostitutes have worked out rationalizations that are at least plausible to themselves even though they are not satisfying to any thoughtful student of humanity's vagaries. And the race-rioter is no exception. While he is an unstable person easily seized upon by emotion and hysteria, it usually takes an actual clash or a lurid story to drive him across the line into anti-social mob activity. The rumors of a fever-heightened verbal milling process furnish him with that justification, with that anesthetic for his conscience, with those "conscience-soothing falsities" of the kind Mark Twain mentions in *The Mysterious Stranger*.

These rumor symptoms circulate with increasing rapidity in barber shops, beauty parlors, bars, church socials, in lobbies, business gatherings, union meetings, and family conclaves, in face-to-face talks, telephone conversations, and even in rare instances over the radio and in the newspapers. Their origins are difficult to locate until one considers the significant fact that on the eve of race riots, rumors frequently bear the earmarks of artificial creation and abnormally rapid dissemination. This brings us to the rumor-mills of demagogic groups, discussed under point 4, below. But before turning to that area for riot symptoms, let us look first at the actual events that serve as storm signals for the coming riot-storm.

3. Racial Frictions

As we have said, race riots are set in motion by a vast number of rumors, personal irritations, and situations adversely affecting the lives of far more people than those who take part in the riots. Imagine the impact of millions of incidents like the following ones told by eye-witnesses, and you will visualize the power of racial frictions; you will come to an appreciation of their role as symptoms:

A fellow was in the theater near me and when the lights went on he saw he was sitting next to a Negro who "smelled so bad" that the man got sick. If the lights would have stayed out, I'll bet the man would never have known that a colored person was sitting next to him.

A Negro woman defense worker came in and asked to see some coats. I saw the clerk bring out several average-priced coats, and the woman soon warned the clerk, "Don't waste my time. This stuff is cheap. Bring me something good!" The customer ended the conversation with the remark, "The Negro is coming into his own now, and he won't lose his gains after the war."

I saw a white man kick a Negro as he got off a street car. The white man claimed that the Negro had pushed him a little, but the white man had actually been making it difficult for the Negro to get off the car.

A white southerner knocked down a Negro in our plant for speaking to a white female employee, saying, "Next time you speak to a girl you better talk to a nigger girl."

A sailor, seeing an argument on a bus between the Negro driver and a white passenger, said, "We know how to handle those birds where I come from," and he held up his neckerchief.

A Negro girl got on the street car and, just as she was sitting down, the car started onward. Losing her balance, she bumped against a white woman sitting next to her. The woman gave the girl a contemptuous glance and muttered, "You clumsy nigger."

The following incidents were reported to an investigator:

White boys at a high school ganging up on the Negroes because they (the Negroes) had excelled in the track meet.

A white streetcar conductor insulting a Negro woman for boarding the car with an invalid transfer: "You niggers are always trying to get away with something."

Loud and insulting remarks by a table of white women as a Negro woman came into a restaurant to eat.

Violent incidents, more closely approximating riot proportions, have dotted Detroit history, especially during the year and one-half before Bloody Monday. Clashes between Negroes and whites occurred many times following riots at the Sojourner Truth Homes in February, 1942. They included the unreported fight early in 1943 near Northwestern High School in which two Negroes were badly beaten and one is reported to have died; student fights and a shot fired near a high school in Ferndale, Detroit suburb; suburban Inkster's clash between white soldiers and groups of Negroes; the recurring Packard strikes with their inter-racial aspects; and the struggles between white and black boys at Eastwood (commercial amusement) Park.

And there are such constant irritants (in Detroit) as a concrete wall one-half mile long, eight feet high, which was constructed in the outskirts of the city between a semi-rural Negro area and suburban homes of whites.

All these things are markings on Detroit's fever chart. Under other place-names, they have their counterparts as indications of the rising fevers elsewhere.

Here again, with respect to the symptoms of an approaching riot, the incidents are not as significant in themselves as is the inescapable fact that they begin to increase in (a) frequency, (b) boldness, and (c) violence.

4. Demagogic Groups

Groups of emotional anti-Negroes and of emotional anti-whites flourish and die out in many American communities. Detroit has had its anti-Negro Christian Fronters who followed Father Charles E. Coughlin of Royal Oak, Michigan, its Ku Klux Klansmen, and its Black Legionnaires. And these organizations still persist. More recently it has also had, among the whites:

Dixie Voters' League
Southern Society of Michigan
United Sons of America
American Mothers
America First Party (formerly Gerald L. K. Smith's "Committee of 1,000,000")
Roseville Riflemen's Association (formerly the National Worker's League)

As an informant told an investigator, "Many of these are passing as decent societies—for example, the United Sons of America and the

Riflemen's Association. The latter holds a charter from a national association which is not anti-Negro. But it seems clear that they have fostered stereotypes which contribute to the rioting."

Detroit's anti-white organizations have until recently included the (Japanese-inspired) Eastern Pacific League, the Moorish Science Temple of Am, the Improvement of Our Own, and the Universal Negro Improvement Association. Informants say that the League was "probably Japanese-inspired," but few know anything about it. One of its signs "was reported as being seen over a store in Paradise Valley, 'The Belgians have 4,000,000 slaves in Belgian Congo.'" The Improvement Association is "the Negro nationalist movement. . . . Their line is one of militancy and aggression. Every white man is a potential enemy. They claim to want eventually a Negro republican Africa."

In searching for symptoms, we must know as much about such anti-democratic organizations as we can, even though it is generally agreed that none of those mentioned actually organized the Bloody Week Riots. These bodies and the anti-Negro, anti-Catholic, and anti-Jewish sermons preached in many of Detroit's fundamentalist churches generated an emotional climate of intolerance and hysteria, of *organizational sanction* for aggressive activities. As an outstanding Negro leader claims:

> The total insecurity in this city can be seen in all the religious groups that have grown up recently. These are the fundamentalists—the 100% American Protestants. They are really preaching the same things as the old organized fascist groups did. They are building up the "right" atmosphere. I don't know whether this is just in Detroit or not—the ads in the Saturday papers now take up nearly two full pages for such churches.

Another religious leader, a white man, tells of the way in which these fundamentalist groups "are becoming centers of influence in the [industrial] plants. They hold informal lunchtime meetings of little groups of fifty sometimes. Some of these leaders are boasting of great success. They all take an anti-Negro line."

In addition to breeding and sanctioning an atmosphere of intolerance, such anti-Negro groups also serve—as we suggested in connection with rumors above—as the rumor-mills and propaganda-mills out of which the intolerant get their ready-made prejudices. Such organizations also provide leaders and rank-and-filers to jump into any riot situation the instant the "break" against law and order has occurred. On the basis of data available up to the present, it is not possible to say that they created Bloody Monday in the sense of planning it in detail and directing it, but it is inescapable that they seized upon a race riot as an opportunity to demonstrate their power.

With respect to symptoms of an impending race riot, the chief thing to look for in connection with such organizations is a progressive tendency to operate more openly and boldly; to propagandize against the Negroes and whites; to presume the existence of a greater degree of social acceptance for their views. This dangerous development among Detroit's demagogic groups pointed directly at impending riots in the minds of many experienced observers. It is a development that must always be watched with care.

5. Juvenile Delinquency

"Many Negroes just the age of those young hoodlums who were most active in the riots," according to the Reverend Horace White, Negro member of the Detroit Housing Commission, "must roam the streets at night because they have no place to sleep." Though this is an exaggerated statement, there is abundant evidence proving that Detroit's 'teen-age youngsters have been turned loose upon the streets in World War II. The city was warned repeatedly by social work leaders and juvenile court spokesmen. Juvenile delinquency among both boys and girls, and especially among the latter, mounted steadily to higher and higher levels in Detroit as in many war-boom cities in 1942-43.

Governor Harry F. Kelly of Michigan pointed to a frightful consequence of such rampant delinquency when he said that "75 percent of all the trouble was due to 'teen-age groups." He called for what most of Detroit's juvenile delinquents, including its youthful rioters, did not have—parental care and supervision. *Life* gave pictures of marching mobs of white youngsters and told how "Detroiters were puzzled and disturbed over the sudden appearance of youthful gangs like this," many members of which were "only 15 or 16." The Negro mobs, with strong zoot-suit sections, were characterized by *Life* and others, and appeared to the authors, to be slightly older than the white, possibly averaging 21 years of age. As evidence of this general contention, A. M. Smith reported in the Detroit *News* that among the first 199 persons arrested by the police were 91 youths, or 45 per cent, who were from 17 to 21 years of age. In view of the tendency of the police to arrest the most available people—the least agile—this percentage is probably misleadingly low.

In many ways, the war situation has aggravated the general condition of family disorganization to which sociologists and social workers have pointed with increasing emphasis for many years. The Nazis and the Fascisti capitalized upon the lack of wisdom with which the Germans and Italians handled their similar youth problems, arising out of similar family disorganization during and after World War I. As Dr. E. Franklin Frazier, noted Negro sociologist of Howard University, states, "To my way of thinking, this presents one of the major problems of our modern urban civilization."

When police reports of arrests of delinquents begin to soar, when social workers learn of more and more children left to fend for themselves while their parents work, an explosion is in the making. The emergence of gangs of 'teen-age hoodlums, of potential thieves, prostitutes, perverts, and gangsters, is a price we do not need to pay as a part of the war effort.

6. Police Behavior

To look for symptoms of forthcoming race riots in police behavior may strike some readers as an impertinent suggestion or, on the contrary, as a proposal that places too much faith upon police wisdom. Neither of these implications is intended. Once one understands the various pressures and motives—personal, political, and communal—involved in a man becoming a policeman, one can learn the kinds of *changes in police behavior* that are storm signals of approaching outbreaks and especially of race riots.

Let us look at some pertinent aspects of police behavior. Army behavior in peacetime presents a rough parallel to police work: both are deadly routines of chores that bring slurs, few commendations, and many other frustrating experiences. Again, these frustrations quite humanly find outlets in domestic fights, brawls, and suicides. War is to the Army much what civilian outbreaks are to the police. Both offer socially acceptable outlets for the residuum of aggressiveness characteristic of each. This suggests one pertinent aspect of police psychology that must be borne in mind when analyzing police behavior.

These psychological "ground swells," so briefly touched upon, lie beneath the riot symptoms. The actual storm warnings are: (1) an increasing distrustfulness of the police by Negroes, usually accompanied by increasing arrests of Negroes, and by more and more strident headlines in the Negro press; (2) evidences of more camaraderie between police and hoodlum elements in the face of a "common threat" to white domination; and (3) a mounting number of accounts of third-degree and other police violence and of disciplinary actions by police officials.

The first kind of symptoms, increasing distrustfulness, takes the form of increasing and urgent demands by Negroes for adequate Negro representation on the police force, for equal treatment of Negro and white prisoners, and for other implementations of the rights guaranteed to citizens under the Federal Constitution.

It is more difficult to gather reports of the second kind of symptoms: camaraderie between police and hoodlum elements in the face of the "Negro threat." It is manifested in bars, pool rooms, bowling alleys, police stations, fire halls. While the police find themselves at odds with strikers because of the police tradition to protect property rights above other rights, they and the hoodlums find security in belonging to "good outfits," in being respected by a lot of the "boys." Thus they naturally welcome a common cause that extends their human connections.

A scout car pulled up to a vacant lot where some Negro children were playing around a bonfire. One of the cops yelled at the kids, "Get out of here, you nigger bastards!"

Some Negro and white boys were fighting. A policeman, who could have known none of the circumstances, came up and seized two of the Negro boys and arrested them. He didn't seem concerned with the white boys.

A teacher was walking with a policeman out of a high school building in the late afternoon. The policeman saw a group of Negro high school students joking with one another and called to them, "Break it up, you black apes!"

These incidents point to the "tough guy" tradition, so valued in police ranks, and they also furnish mild examples of the sort of bullying that is an evidence of a riot in the making. In a sense, the more overt the "tough guy" behavior becomes toward the racial minority, the greater a contribution the police will make to the precipitation of a race riot. As the Detroit situation well illustrated, too, the police were not alone in believing that "strong-arm" tactics would have merit. Both citizen leaders and groups demanded many times that the announced "kid gloves" policy of the Mayor and the Police Commissioner in handling race clashes should be discarded for more "decisive measures," presumably to "keep the Negroes in their place."

When anti-Negro bullying becomes more overt, when the Negroes give evidences of a rising fear of the police—in short, when police-Negro relations assume feud proportions—the danger signals are flying. And these symptoms are stimulated by factors discussed in the next two groups: overcrowding and employment.

7. Overcrowding

When real estate boards issue reports about the urgent need for laws to protect "restricted" (*viz.*, white) housing developments, one must recognize that on the other side of the picture are such situations as the following, written by an informant:

> Leo, a colored washer in a Detroit defense plant, told me that he pays twelve dollars a week for two rooms behind a store. The roof leaks, and he has to sleep on the floor in the kitchen to keep from getting soaked during the rain. A request to his landlord for repairs brought him the information that if he didn't like his place to try and get another one.

Another example was given of apartments rented originally to white occupants for $25.00 *a month* that were "converted" to colored occupancy and then in 1943 rented to Negroes at from $15.00 to $18.00 *a week.*

In other words, as these incidents suggest, overcrowding in a city focuses immediate attention in the race field upon two opposing processes: (1) a tremendous accumulation of pressures within the hemmed-in Negro districts is expressed in terms of high rents, bad facilities, and insolent landlords; (2) sharp defensive movements on the part of the landlords and real estate interests strive to keep the Negro community from expanding in directions where they fear that Negro occupancy would lower property values. Watch these movements—both the Negro-expansive and the white-restrictive ones— because their increasing aggressiveness and urgency are forerunners of race riots.

By overcrowding we naturally do not refer to housing facilities alone. The overcrowding of recreation and transportation facilities is usually a concomitant of the housing situation. Msgr. Francis J. Haas, Chairman of the U. S. Fair Employment Practice Committee, has said that the responsibility for the Detroit race riots may be attributed to "inadequate housing, recreation, and public transportation."

Negroes and whites who lived as neighbors did not fight one another in the Detroit race riots. They had come to know and to understand each other. But Negroes and whites who felt the pressure and competition of each other's group for *Lebensraum* (living space)

—to borrow an appropriate German word—and who were not prepared to solve their problems co-operatively, these folks had a tendency to resort to the futile tactic of blaming one another. They were blaming each other for a situation for which neither was to blame. Such mutual abuse is a symptom of grave significance.

8. Employment

"Of course you're going to have trouble. If you can keep them stupid and dumb, you can keep them in their place. Just let them start thinking that they're smart, and you'll never be able to hold the jigs down again."

This is the ancient theory of social control utilized by authoritarians everywhere, a theory against which advocates of democracy have fought for centuries. It is here given as restated by a Detroit real estate operator. It is the attitude that led, in early June, 1943, to the strike of 3,000 or more white and Negro Packard workers over the upgrading of three skilled Negro employees, an upgrading to which union contracts had entitled them. The strike affected in all about 20,000 Packard employees. It is also a statement that points vividly to the same kind of internal and external tensions to which we made reference in the foregoing discussion of overcrowding. Negroes naturally want to get the recognition and other benefits to which equivalent labor and skill entitle white workers. They claim such rights with less patience as pressure against them increases. The whites, on the other hand, and especially those whites who have not learned to solve racial problems in co-operation with the colored people, regard every advance of the Negroes as a threat to white prestige and economic security as expressed in white control of jobs. They remember the months and perhaps years during which Depression and Recession made their livelihood uncertain. And they are quick to meet the Negro "threat" with the only tactics they know: kicking the Negro "back into his place." To this, Walter White of the N.A.A.C.P. adds, "Negroes were still unemployed while Detroit employers were industriously recruiting white labor, chiefly in the South."

Here are some of the "ifs" to regard as dangerous: (1) *if* previously destitute Negroes start getting "big money," especially plentiful money that can be spent only in a few limited but public areas; (2) *if* the normal channels of collective bargaining are closed or seriously impaired so that industrial unrest has no normal means of expression and outlet but is diverted into kicking the Negro around as a scape-goat; (3) *if* more and more Negroes and whites must be thrown into employment contact with one another without adequate preparation for working together sensibly and democratically—if these things exist, then watch for trouble! Serious racial antagonisms are in the making.

If These Symptoms Appear

Sociologists cannot, in all honesty, construct as yet mathematical formulas with which to predict race riots or—for that matter—any other human event. Neither do they believe that race riots can be blamed upon single causes; they realize that race riots, like practically all human events, derive from a multiplicity of causes, many of which are hard to isolate. But they can point to dangerous symptoms, such as we are doing, and thus furnish a means of estimating the nearness of the actual "blow-off." It necessarily takes interest and experience and courage to put this knowledge into action.

With these precautions in mind, we can say, *Watch for these symptoms of race riots in the making:*

1. A shift in the climate of opinion that will permit sadistic and aggressive *sentiments* to find expression, that will permit hidden hatreds against the Negroes and against the whites to replace the tolerant *opinions* that society ordinarily maintains.

2. An increase in the speed of race-rumor circulation and in the purposiveness and the sensational character of the rumors.

3. Intensification in the (a) frequency, (b) boldness, and (c) violence of racial frictions.

4. A progressive tendency upon the part of anti-Negro (and anti-white) organizations, including extremist and fundamentalist religious sects, to propagandize against the Negroes (and the whites) more openly, to presume the existence of a greater degree of social accept-ance than they had had.

5. Spectacular rises in the juvenile delinquency rate as revealed in arrests and social-work records.

6. An increasing distrustfulness of the police by Negroes, usually accompanied by increasing arrests and bullying of Negroes. The Negro press is useful on this point even though it often tends to sensationalize.

7. Evidences of a common front of pro-white and anti-Negro camaraderie between the police and hoodlum elements.

8. Increasingly prominent accounts of third-degree and other police violence in general and of disciplinary actions by police officials.

9. An accumulation of pressures for living space within a hemmed-in Negro district, expressed in terms of exorbitant rents, inadequate living facilities, and unconcerned landlords.

10. Sharp defensive movements on the part of the landlords and real estate people to keep the Negro community from expanding in directions where they believe Negro occupancy would lower property values.

11. White envy of "big money" now earned by formerly impoverished Negroes who do not know how to handle it and who naturally spend it rather openly.

12. Factors that clog or seriously impair the normal and accepted channels of collective bargaining so that industrial unrest has no adequate means of expression and outlet and thus may be diverted into anti-Negro excesses.

13. Increases in Negro and white employment contact where there has not been adequate preparation for sensible and democratic association.

Not all of these symptoms may appear as forerunners of a race riot. None of these symptoms alone would probably point to danger sufficiently serious to call out the State Militia. But every one of these symptoms points to danger spots that may grow and breed additional danger spots. Every one of these symptoms, as it emerges, demands immediate and decisive attention.

Chapter 10

TAKE THE FOLLOWING
ACTIONS:

TO prevent race riots, one must do more than know and be able to
recognize their symptoms. In Detroit, after all, as a highly competent analyst of the situation, William H. Baldwin (President,
National Urban League), put it, "The whole community, white and
Negro, knew for a matter of years that a tinder box was in the making;
but, although surveys and reports were made and handed around,
no responsible individuals or agencies—public or private—provided
any persistent and effective follow-through. It was pretty much a
'business as usual' psychology on the part of all concerned."

To prevent race riots, one must do more than "establish a co-
ordinating organization and get co-operation." Detroit had a promising
plan and a Mayor's Race Committee seventeen years before Bloody
Monday, 1943, but it did not have the "persistent and effective follow-
through" to which Mr. Baldwin refers. It did not treat the threat of
race disorders in the way in which we treat the more remote threat
of air raids in World War II.

As a result of the Detroit race riot of 1925, which followed the
purchase of a house in a white district by Dr. Ossian Sweet, a Negro
physician, Detroit's first Mayor's Race Committee came into existence.
Rev. Reinhold Niebuhr, now of the Union Theological Seminary, New
York, and Bishop William T. Vernon, of the African Methodist
Episcopal Church, headed this group as Chairman and Vice-Chairman,
respectively. This committee, as its comprehensive report on recommendations indicates, "arrived at many specific recommendations involving official policy and governmental action" even though it had

to realize that "the final solution of all the problems which have been revealed must await upon the cultivation of better understanding and the diminution of prejudice in the public at large." Even though this committee urged "a permanent race commission" and many effective measures, Detroit persisted in its "business as usual" psychology through large and small riots and other disorders, climaxed by the riots at the Sojourner Truth Houses in 1942, the strikes at the Packard plant, and then the riots throughout a large area of the city on Bloody Monday in 1943.

How many race riots must Detroit suffer before it adopts a program of prevention? What kind of a program of prevention is indicated by Detroit's experiences? What can American cities—Detroit included—learn from the Siege of Paradise Valley in late June, 1943?

In working out a program of race-riot prevention for American cities, the authors of this book are well aware that no panacea can be offered for so complex a problem. We do not, therefore, propose a rigid and all-inclusive plan. We are, rather, offering here an outline and description of steps that can be taken by any city to combat the creeping horror of race riots.

The suggested steps given in this chapter should not be viewed as being merely the opinions of the authors. On the contrary, they represent a composite product, based upon the actual experiences of a great many individuals and organizations in a number of civic and political fields and in many cities, as revealed in interviews and in confidential and published reports. In addition, the authors themselves have experimented with similar techniques of civic organization nationally and in a half-dozen American cities.

The specific projects that we mention should be adapted to the scope, finances, and specific needs of each city that has a race-tensions problem. Some of the program steps mentioned are not necessary in many cities. For example, suitable information essential to an approach to the problem may already exist, collected in a satisfactory manner by existing agencies. In such a case, comprehensive new fact-finding efforts would serve no useful purpose.

At the outset, we must also recognize that a program to prevent race riots has more immediate objectives and problems than a program to bring about mutually satisfactory bi-racial relationships. For practical purposes, therefore, this chapter is divided into these four parts:

1. What to do to prevent race riots
2. What not to do if you want to prevent race riots

3. If the riot breaks out anyway, do these things—quickly
4. How to change basic anti-Negro and anti-white patterns.

The discussion of each of these points is meant to be primarily practical rather than philosophical or academic or comprehensive. For the more subtle and complex aspects of this entire subject, we refer you to titles listed in the final section of this book, "Suggested Readings."

1. WHAT TO DO TO PREVENT RACE RIOTS

Cities with bi-racial* problems need two organizations to work out and implement a Race Riot Prevention program comparable to a well-developed Air Raid Precautions system. These may well take the following forms:

1. *An official bi-racial commission appointed by the Governor or Mayor.* This body should have sufficient power and budget to serve as a means for co-ordinating these facilities of governmental agencies: *a.* fact-finding (social workers, police, court system, investigators attached to other departments); *b.* analytical (executives and experts serving the appropriate departments); and *c.* implementational (all facilities—legislative, judicial, and administrative—capable of carrying out constructive inter-racial measures).

2. *A civic bi-racial committee sponsored by leading civic, labor, religious, business, and educational bodies.* This organization can have the advantages of flexibility and informality usually impossible in a governmental instrument, and it can effectively organize citizen pressure behind the constructive projects of the commission, against its political enemies, and also against efforts within the commission to return to a "business as usual" psychology.

Both bodies must be strongly bi-racial in membership as well as in point of view, with practical Negro members who represent actual Negro interests, not so-called "white-man Negroes," and with practical white members who have a vivid appreciation of the crucial nature of white-Negro frictions. In other words, the following recent personal report and analysis by a Chicago newspaperman should be heeded:

Chicago's Mayor has appointed the usual committee of well-wishers and idealists in an alleged attempt to try to prevent race riots here. Such people are fine in analyzing *after the fact* how situations arose and what should

---

*In our use of the term, bi-racial, no connotation of Negro and white separatism or segregation is intended. It is meant to convey the impression of representation and integration, not of distinction and caste.

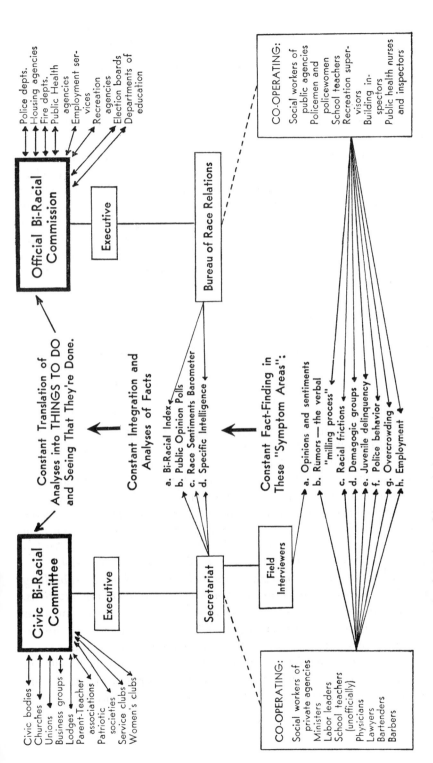

PROPOSED CHART OF ORGANIZATION AND FUNCTION

have been done to prevent them, but I have no confidence in them to prevent anything. . . .

In cases of this sort politicians decide to be "on the level" and think they accomplish this by putting in idealists and "good people" when what they need are the so-called practical people whom they ordinarily use at other times.

Few white men can recognize and select Negro leaders in a manner satisfactory to the Negroes themselves because Negroes select their own leaders on the basis of somewhat different criteria. As Roi Ottley states in his book about his people, *New World A-Coming* (1943), "the day has passed when a white man can choose the Negro's political leaders." Negroes want, above all, Negro leaders that represent first of all Negro interests; if such leaders are also *persona grata* to the whites, the Negroes do not object, but they want no more "Uncle Toms."

In addition to such problems of organization membership, it is also well to stress the reasons for recommending the organization of both a governmental commission and a civic committee. This common dual form of organization is urged because the governmental commission may have prestige and power in the government but be politically handicapped in carrying on propaganda activities. The civic committee, on the other hand, even though it lacks governmental power, can organize educational and pressure activities that will probably be essential to the success of any race-riot prevention program.

Both the official bi-racial commission and the civic bi-racial committee should also be given adequate legal and budgetary support. They qualify for prestige and influence to the same extent as other bodies confronting "continuous emergencies"—police, fire, city planning, and education commissions and boards. In any city with a sizable and unassimilated Negro population, the time to establish such twin organizations is—as soon as possible. *Do not wait until your city has sacrificed citizens to mob violence in its first or second race riot.*

And both bodies should stand "on their own" and not be subsidiary to other comparable government commissions and civic organizations. If they are to serve their necessary purposes, they must remain as independent and free to act as possible. To assure friendly co-ordination, they should have certain influential members in common.

Above all, each of the organizations should equip itself with an executive who understands that "committees do not work," that committee members talk a lot, tell others what to do, and only occasionally undertake small assignments. But the executive must understand that the real labor of accomplishment is *his*. He has to realize that it is up to him and his staff to learn how to function in the name of and through the medium of the civic committee or governmental commission for which he works. Such an executive will naturally also be a man who has had practical organizational and publicity experience in some such field as newspaper work, ward politics, salesmanship, or advertising. This will give him the essential grasp of the public relations implications of his program. Without such a grasp, many civic and governmental projects fail.

The program for these two organizations, to be divided between them operationally or handled jointly as seems wisest in terms of support and available personnel, must include three main functions, as follows:

1. *Constant fact-finding*
2. *Constant integration and analysis of facts*
3. *Constant translation of analyses into* THINGS TO DO

As these points suggest, the *time element* is as crucial in combating race riots as it is in any dynamic public relations program formed to counteract emotional excesses. It has been said that eternal vigilance is the price of safety, and it is certainly true that eternal vigilance is the price of freedom from riots.

But let us try to lift these three main program elements out of the realm of generality and suggest some specific content for a constructive and persistent program:

1. Constant Fact-Finding

Essential to any anti-race-riot program is an accurate and constant "feel of the pulse" of Negro-white tensions. Without accurate first-hand reports, wishful thinking and prejudiced planning all too readily begin to flourish. This "feel of the pulse" cannot be furnished by any one agency because organizational and political quirks tend to characterize and even to distort the information obtained through any single set of channels.

An example will clarify this principle. A riotous mob of 400 threatened twenty-nine Negroes graduating from Detroit's large Northeastern High School the second night after Bloody Monday. Nevertheless, Police Commissioner John H. Witherspoon released to the newspapers a precinct report to the effect that his police handled a crowd of

"50 to 60 youths between the ages of 15 and 20" in a routine fashion, without excitement and *without aid from soldiers.* Previous to the Commissioner's statement, however, the morning Detroit *Free Press,* on the basis of staff writer Lyford Moore's information, ran an eight-column headline on page one thus: "TROOPS FOIL GRADUATION RIOT: *Class Is Escorted Past Milling Mob: Northeastern Students Taken Home Under Guard of Soldiers' Bayonets.*" Walter P. Reuther, Vice-President of the United Automobile Workers' Union (C.I.O.), who spoke at the graduation exercises, verified the *Free Press* account on the basis of his own observation of the work of Federal soldiers.

From this example, it is obvious that the "feel of the pulse" should be taken by a *variety of kinds of reporters* so that a dependable check may be obtained. They should also be informants who have normal functions that bring them constantly into intimate contact with people scattered through a variety of occupations. They should also be so chosen that their contacts will assure geographic, economic, and social cross-sections of the city's population. Such a reportorial machinery should therefore assure frequent and frank reports from selected social workers, ministers, policemen and policewomen, labor leaders, school teachers, physicians, bartenders, barbers, recreation supervisors, judges, and others who have immediate and candid contacts with leaders and rank-and-filers among whites and blacks.

As the organizational chart on page 123 indicates, certain aspects of the reportorial function may well be canalized through a bureau under the direction of the official bi-racial commission, and others may best clear through the office force of the non-official bi-racial committee. Such governmental functionaries as social workers, policemen, police-women, school teachers, recreation supervisors, building inspectors, and health inspectors furnish reports on conditions to their supervisors which can be made.to include more adequate and specific information on Negro conditions and Negro-white relations. These governmental reports, clearing through the appropriate channels, can then be made available as a part of official routine—at least in summary form—to the official bureau of race relations and there "processed" to create the crystallizations discussed as part of the second function of the twin organizations. On the other hand, the secretariat of the civic bi-racial committee may arrange to obtain frequent reports from these unofficial co-operators: private social workers, labor leaders, ministers, school teachers working in an unofficial capacity, physicians, lawyers, bar-

tenders, barbers, and a group of trained and paid public opinion interviewers.

These reports from *unofficial sources* of this kind will have the two
merits of (1) supplying a check upon the official facts and assessments, and (2) of furnishing less formal and probably more incisive
insights into evolving tendencies. The specific kinds of reports that
should be received from the groups of informants are, in general, those
set forth in the previous chapter as eight areas of symptoms of the
riot virus. These areas are: (1) opinions and sentiments, (2) rumors—
the verbal "milling process," (3) racial frictions, (4) demagogic
groups, (5) juvenile delinquency, (6) police behavior, (7) overcrowding, and (8) employment. The formulations required for reports on
these symptoms will be apparent from our discussion of the second
program element.

2. Constant Integration and Analysis of Facts

The reports obtained directly or through supervisors in summary
form would be such that the official bureau of race relations and the
unofficial secretariat may be able to make them contribute to one or
more of four kinds of generalizations. These generalizations may be:

a. *Bi-Racial Indexes.* (These assessments may be prepared by
the official bureau of race relations from official reports.) Through the
use of statistics on arrests, reported difficulties on buses, streetcars, in
stores and restaurants, in schools and factories, records of industrial
absentees and school truancies, and similar developments, an index can
be established that will give a rough composite "reading" on the comparative calmness or feverishness of the bi-racial situation at frequent
intervals. If staff and funds are available, this device would be made
more useful by preparing Bi-Racial Indexes for each area of the city
so that the fever-spots may be localized and may be related more easily
and directly to local problems of immigration, housing, employment,
antagonistic sentiments, and the like.

b. *Public Opinion Polls.* (These measurements may be prepared
by the unofficial secretariat.) While public opinion polls yield merely
a report on "surface reactions" to questions put by a stranger, they do
measure the extent to which race tensions under such conditions are
being verbalized in public. With such qualifications, discussed in detail
in the preceding chapter (9), opinion polls can furnish a useful "run-

ning check" on developments, in terms of such significant social group-
ings as area, employment, age, sex, religion, and race. Naturally, great
care needs to be exercised in the construction and pre-testing of questions and in the selection and training of interviewers as well as in
the mechanics of sampling. Fortunately in many cities fairly adequate
organizations exist through which interviewing services may be ob-
tained· at less cost than would be involved in setting up one's own
system. Such an arrangement has, however, the disadvantage of making one dependent upon the relatively untrained interviewers found in
many such organizations, interviewers lacking especially in the psychological training that would permit them to aid materially in the next
type of generalization.

c. *Race Sentiments Barometer.* (This estimate of tensions may be
prepared by civic committee's secretariat, subject to criticisms and suggestions from the official bureau of race relations and its supervising
commission.) In addition to the statistical materials summarized in the
Bi-Racial Indexes and Public Opinion Polls, competent reporters will
be able to send in shrewd qualitative estimates of popular sentiments
and tensions that should give more adequate assessments of bi-racial
tendencies than either the Index or the Polls. Such a Race Sentiments
Barometer, quantitatively rough though it must be, can estimate the
intensity of emotional drives, and this will furnish a dimension not
revealed by either the Index or the Polls. The Index, in other words,
can be used to sum up the current behavior situation; the Polls can
summarize verbal reactions to Negro-white situations; the Race Sentiments Barometer can give a basis for more fundamental diagnosis and
more accurate prediction through determining the power of the emotional drives at work, the significance of the societal and psychological
"ground swells."

d. *Specific Intelligence.* (This may be assembled by both the official
race relations bureau and the secretariat of the civic bi-racial committee.) In addition to these over-all assessments of mass behavior and
emotion, information should be compiled continuously on the specific
program activities of anti-white and anti-Negro leaders and organizations. When they give out statements, picket Negro or white meetings,
organize publicity efforts, start to expand their organizations, or whatever, *immediate estimates* of the effect and success of such actions should
be made available to those who are entrusted with implementation
efforts, with those involved in *Constant translation of analyses into*
THINGS TO DO, as discussed below. In addition to the immediate use

of such reports (frequently not of sufficient news significance to reach the pages of newspapers), they should be suitably filed by whichever organization collected them (or both) in order to give a more and more detailed picture of the prejudicial activities of intolerant and subversive white and Negro leaders and groups. It is quite possible that some such dossiers will eventually accumulate and present a composite perspective that none of the individual items could reveal: a picture of anti-social activity sufficiently damning to warrant legal indictment and trial.

Through these four types of summaries, the two organizations may have in effect a fever chart of the city, a chart that could not only guide their efforts but also the more long-term Negro-white projects to which reference is made at the end of this chapter. But, as we said at the outset, facts are not enough for riot-prevention purposes. What can we *do* with such information once we have it at our fingertips? Let us set forth at least a few of the effective things that we can *do* to offset riots:

3. Constant Translation of Analyses into THINGS TO DO

This significant program function is also the one on which we are most likely to fall down. People like to talk. Under compulsion, they will consent to gather facts and even permit the facts gathered to have some influence upon their opinions, especially if that influence cannot be interpreted as an opinion change in a "face-losing" sense. But once we get that far, the next step is likely to fall short of real implementation in any effective sense. It usually amounts to nothing more than passing a resolution or writing a memo that will *ask someone else or some other organization* to do the necessary job. This resolution or memo then permits us to feel that we have "done our duty" and to blame any bad consequences on the fact that the receivers of our suggestions neither liked to be given suggestions nor to do anything effective!

For our present purposes, we shall have to assume that the organizations involved are sufficiently earnest in their desire to eliminate race disorders that they will provide the "persistent and effective follow-through" that Mr. Baldwin did not find in Detroit. We shall also assume that the members of the organizations will not waste time futilely on discussing the "relative merits" in the direction of their policy-making of segregation as opposed to gradual democratic assimilation. Candid students of the white-Negro situation in the United States generally agree that segregation ceased to be practical one day in the summer of 1619 when Negroes first stepped ashore as slaves in Jamestown, Virginia. The impact of the Negro upon American culture and the proportion of mulattoes in the American population demonstrate the cultural and physiological futility of all artificial restraints upon intermingling. We must also remember that the blind hate of intolerance is a product not of association but of what sociologists call "social distance." Let us never lose sight of three great lessons of the Detroit tragedy! People who had become neighbors in mixed Negro and white neighborhoods did not riot against each other. The students of Wayne University—white and black—went to their classes in peace throughout Bloody Monday. And there were no disorders between the white and black workers in the war plants, according to U. S. Attorney General Francis Biddle and to Major General Henry S. Aurand of the U. S. Army.

Rather than to such an oversimplified "solution" as segregation, one must look to a vast number of expedient *adjustments* through which to combat race frictions. Through adjusting situations here and there with as much wisdom as possible, through handling case after case as it arises, the tensions between the races may be eased and offset, eventually relaxed and removed, and healthier patterns of race contact may be fostered.

Without more ado concerning the nature of what we should do to ease tensions, let us turn to the ways in which a public relations program for the lessening of race frictions can be implemented. The actions we recommend fall into these general categories: for the official commission, (a) requests for official action, and (b) publicity; for the unofficial civic committee, (c) public education, (d) pressure activities, and (e) bi-racial experiences.

a. *Requests for Official Action.* Because of its official position, the bi-racial commission can make requests, complaints, and prepare directives that will command consideration within the city government and in other governmental circles, consideration that the resolutions of the civic committee cannot command. Such requests will naturally be as multifarious as are the necessary and expedient adjustments in race relations. They will involve projects ranging from the construction of public housing to the proper enforcement of some relatively minor city ordinance. Proposals for official action originating in the civic committee may, in many cases, appropriately be referred first to the official bi-racial commission.

b. and c. *Publicity and Public Education.* (To be handled by the official commission and the civic committee, with activities divided between them or carried on jointly as seems most wise. The antipathy in certain circles to "official propaganda" of any sort naturally must be taken into consideration.) Through such channels as daily and weekly newspapers, radio stations, schools, churches, women's and men's clubs, labor unions, publicity materials concerning race relations should be given virtually incessant dissemination. This mass-distribution of facts cannot be achieved merely through throwing memos into the laps of editors, teachers, preachers, and program-makers. We must realize that the race relations message must compete with dozens of other messages, many of them nearer and dearer to the tastes of our hoped-for public education media. To be assured of an adequate and reasonably continual acceptance of our messages, we must translate them into the forms most easily usable by our proposed media.

Daily and weekly newspapers want well-written accurate news stories from dependable sources that they can insert into their columns with a minimum of editing. They also want the "stuff" out of which editorial writers, columnists, and feature writers can easily create the kind of articles *they want to write.* Radio stations do not want speeches, except in rare cases; they want attractive programs or inserts for existing programs that will make people want to stay tuned to their wave length. Schools want timely teaching aids that will fit into existing courses, that will help their teachers do a better job with the mental and physical equipment they possess. Schools and churches, unions and clubs can also be induced to utilize speakers whom they can schedule, preferably in advance, and whom they can trust to present before their respective pupils, parishioners, and members an "acceptable message."

Frequent opportunities present themselves for passing on bi-racial information and ideas for action to those who can go out and transmit them to great numbers of other people. Immediate examples are teacher-training colleges, teachers' institutes, program-making conferences for club leaders, special short courses and the like for ministers, real estate operators, insurance salesmen, and others. Suitable program materials can be offered free or at a nominal price, in order to obtain widespread distribution of the message. Such materials may well include posters, play scripts, games, pamphlets, slide films, and, if possible, motion pictures. Through these media, whites in particular can be given what they sadly lack: a faithful and intimate picture of Negroes; and both groups should be presented with the real challenges to inter-racial understanding.

To get the most effective inter-racial understanding in the areas in which it is most needed, education and publicity efforts must also reach "the lower depths" of a community. In other words, means must be found to combat intolerance in the less "genteel" pool rooms, saloons, "social clubs," and other "joints." These are the places where potentially the most riotous elements congregate. Possibly manufacturers of alcoholic beverages and chewing tobaccos will be willing to co-operate in a local campaign of propaganda favorable to bi-racial understanding.

d. *Pressure Activities.* To combat riots, we must learn how to turn organizational pressures powerfully into focus so as to direct them towards the accomplishment of needed objectives. Such pressures are useful to overcome the apathy of governmental agencies; to demonstrate to the community that anti-Negro and anti-white leaders and groups do not represent majority opinions and interests and even constitute dangers to the American way of life; and to obtain financial support for constructive programs.

The organization of such group pressures is best handled—for the sake of effectiveness and flexibility—by the civic committee and involves more than the simple expedient of sending a letter to the presidents of a list of clubs and asking for "suitable action." Your project— a slum-clearance, recreational, police, or possibly a legislative measure —literally needs to be "sold" to the organizations in question; this "sales work" can be done most efficiently as a part of a constant educational campaign that must have been in operation for a reasonable period of time before an actual request for pressure-support is made. When such assurance of support and interest has been prepared, it should be possible to get barrages of wires or letters to legislators or other governmental functionaries; to arrange impressive delegations to attend hearings or to wait upon officials; to bring about the passage of publicity-creating resolutions when such actions are indicated as desirable ones by the circumstances; to get financial aid; or to do whatever else may be indicated.

e. *Bi-racial Experiences.* Possibly the most dramatic kind of implementation for a bi-racial program is one that builds on this homely truth exemplified in the Detroit race riots of the week of June 20, 1943: *Neighbors—black and white—do not riot against each other.* This principle has been utilized in another area by the National Conference of Christians and Jews, its demonstrations of the dramatic educational value of its "trialogue teams." These teams consist of a Roman Catholic priest, a Jewish rabbi, and a Protestant clergyman or of similarly representative laymen. These men speak together before wide ranges of audiences—in schools, public auditoriums, before clubs, labor unions, churches, lodges, civic associations and over the radio—and thus help to give people of our different religious faiths favorable experiences in the human qualities of those professing other faiths. Similarly dramatic *bi-racial* teams would furnish a way of giving white and Negro audiences better opportunities to come into contact with outstanding people of the other race on terms of simple and effective equality and respect.

Other types of bi-racial experiences can also be arranged. They should all have as their goal the synthesis of neighborly attitudes for large numbers of people. They may well include joint meetings of Negro and white organizations—young people's groups, lodges, women's clubs, service bodies—with a Negro or white group serving as host and the other group providing dramatic or musical entertainment. Such joint acts as inter-racial dinners and celebrations of the Holy Communion have been tried in certain cities, but they have not reached wide enough acceptance as yet. And this seems odd, especially in the case of the Lord's Supper.

Among the most practical bi-racial associations are those made necessary by the conditions of employment. Employers, labor leaders, and joint employer-employee committees have done spectacular work in certain industries and cities in creating conditions that brought about the employment of whites and Negroes with a minimum of friction and with resulting inter-racial neighborliness. In spite of the anti-Negro strike at the Detroit Packard plant early in June, 1943—a situation responsibly attributed to Ku Klux Klan agitation—many leaders from other walks of life as well as the general-circulation newspapers commented favorably on the results during the Bloody Monday riots of tolerance-producing experiences and education in the factories and in union ranks. An aggressive program of inter-racial co-operation upon the part of the Greater New York Industrial Union Council and of such specific unions as the United Electrical, Radio & Machine Workers, the Transport Workers, and the National Maritime Union, and of the

Harlem-Riverside C.I.O. Community Council all bore fruit in the inter-racial union campaign to stop the Harlem "Negro Uprising" of 1943. The A.F. of L. Restaurant & Hotel Workers and the C.I.O. Federal Workers have also demonstrated in Washington the value of their work in the promotion of co-operation and in the prevention of inter-racial clashes in that tense city.

For the sake of clarity, let us now summarize here the major steps to be taken to prevent race riots:

1. Prevail upon the Governor or Mayor to set up an official bi-racial commission of effective leaders to work within the governmental struc-ture. See that this commission has a competent executive who under-stands both governmental organization and public relations techniques. (See diagram, page 123.)

2. Set up a strong independent bi-racial committee, or, if practical, strengthen an existing bi-racial organization. Such an organization will have the advantages of flexibility and informality and of being able to organize pressures to compel official actions. See that this committee has a competent executive who understands how committees function, how civic organizations can achieve program objectives, and how public relations problems are handled. (See diagram, page 123.)

3. Through both of these organizations—co-operatively or sepa-rately—report and check constantly

    (a) opinions, sentiments, and tensions affecting Negro-white relations

    (b) incidents of race frictions

    (c) basic factors in living and working that make for tensions, and

    (d) intelligence on anti-Negro and anti-white agitators and organizations.

4. Through the two organizations, work out simplified and effective means—such as a Bi-racial Index, Public Opinion Polls, a Race Sentiments Barometer, and a fund of specific intelligence—for integrat-ing and assessing the information gathered. If there is a division of this labor between the organizations, each should continue to maintain effective checks on the accuracy and comprehensiveness of the other's work.

5. Reject all panaceas as impractical. Segregation in particular must be rejected at the outset, since the only practical preventive course is one involving thousands of workable adjustments which will

in effect implement the Golden Rule and permit the growth of healthy race relations.

6. Emphasize persisting action in the entire program for the prevention of race riots; constantly translate facts and analyses into THINGS TO DO—and see that they are done.

7. In the THINGS TO DO, include especially
>   (a) the organization of the constructive pressures of the community to build sound program projects and to counteract anti-Negro and anti-white efforts, and
>   (b) the dramatization of sound race relations through a program of public education and bi-racial experiences such as we suggest above.

2. WHAT NOT TO DO IF YOU WANT TO PREVENT RACE RIOTS

Naturally the things not to do in a riot-prevention program include the converses of the things to do, but there are a few points that should be stressed in particular, points that perhaps are not as obvious as they might seem to be.

1. *Do not expect to gain much through experimental legislation.* The laws on race and civil disorders in most of our states are fairly satisfactory from the standpoint of meeting race crises, but *the real problem is to obtain adequate and humane law enforcement.*

2. *Do not try to go "too far" or "too fast"—or too slowly.* All effective adjustments of human relations must take into account the *possibilities —what can be done—*in your city. You must work with and through other community leaders, and through them you must reach and obtain the support and sympathy of powerful segments of the community. Programs that *sound* too radical, that bring forward too many new features at once and without adequate preparation, and that require greater speed than the community will sanction—such programs may do more to harm than to aid your riot-elimination program. Temper your procedures to the "readings" of your Bi-Racial Index, Public Opinion Polls, and especially Race Sentiments Barometer.

3. *Do not ignore the less cultured and even the stupid and depraved elements of your city.* These are the people who may terrify you in the next race riot. What they think, what they do with their time, what can be done to restrain or neutralize their anti-Negro and anti-white feelings, should be primary concerns of an anti-race-riot program.

4. *Do not ignore existing bi-racial organizations, especially if they have healthy roots.* The promoters of a riot-prevention program can save themselves a lot of groundwork and the antagonisms likely to arise from duplication by pumping new life into an existing civic or governmental organization rather than by setting up a competing new one. This does not mean, naturally, that an unworkable program with incompetent functionaries should be perpetuated. Investigate the existing foundations and build upon them, if possible.

5. *Beware of excessive fact-finding.* From the time of the Dr. Ossian Sweet race riots in 1925, Detroit has had a lot of fact-finding surveys and program making, but the 1943 race riots demonstrated how little the surveys had accomplished. As an investigator of the 1943 Detroit riots put it, "We cannot make surveys and recommendations and be content to have them gather dust in someone's files." *Fact-finding must be made functional.* It must contribute to a program and should result in modifications of our current thinking and in specific actions. It should not be carried on in an academic spirit of "learning more and more about less and less" if the objective is to prevent race riots and not merely to write a learned disquisition.

6. *Beware of the "committee-appointing dodge."* When politicians or university presidents or other human leaders find themselves compelled to *do* something, they have one all-too-infallible "out": They can appoint a committee. With some judgment in the selection of committee personnel, the group appointed can either accomplish a great deal, or it can stall along for any suitable period and *prevent decisive action* until a time more expedient politically. This point re-emphasizes recommendations made earlier in this chapter.

7. *Beware of complacency, of "business as usual."* Race relations represent a continuing problem in many parts of the United States. To ignore the implications of this problem solves nothing. Leaving the field to the agitations of pro-white whites and pro-Negro Negroes can lead to nothing but bloody outbreaks. Above all, each city that has bi-racial problems ought to take definite precautionary measures of the sort recommended here and then proceed with the business of improving basic Negro and bi-racial conditions in the housing, recreational, employment and other fields.

8. *Beware of emergency-mindedness.* Even though race riots present themselves as emergencies, they are in turn symptoms of deep and abiding American problems that are fundamental. To try to cope with

race riots on the basis of a temporary campaign to meet a passing crisis is to be tragically superficial.

3. IF THE RIOT BREAKS OUT ANYWAY, DO THESE THINGS—QUICKLY!

But, in spite of all your efforts, the race riot may break out anyway. Few can get as much support for their bi-racial tolerance work as it merits. There are, after all, so many human problems that compete for attention, especially among white people, and these are the people who can easily remain the most complacent about bi-racial irritations.

What can a community do to help combat a race riot once the fighting has broken out? Here are a few suggestions:

1. *Demand the state militia or the U. S. Army; do not count on the local police to quell the riots.* At any rate, the police are not likely to handle the situation in an equable fashion. As William H. Baldwin, of the National Urban League, concluded in his confidential report on the Detroit Bloody Week Riots to the League Board (quoted by permission):

From all except official accounts, the police behaved with deplorable stupidity and callousness. Although specific charges must necessarily await official investigation and sifting, the whole trend of eye-witness reports would indicate that they shot to kill on suspicion of looting in the Negro districts, that some of them stood by passively when Negroes were being beaten and killed in the white districts, and that they publicly insulted decent and innocent Negroes whom they were sent to protect. A disturbing phase of the aftermath of the active rioting were the "white papers" issued by the Police Commissioner and subsequently by the Mayor, in which the police performance was praised.

2. *Take immediate steps to have the race riot area quarantined.* New recruits and supplies for the rioters must be kept from reaching them. In taking such precautions, it is naturally also necessary to take steps to protect innocent people in the quarantined areas as soon as possible and to see to it that they receive necessary food and emergency medical care.

3. *Keep the children in school, overtime if necessary, especially in the high schools.* Estimates attribute from one-third to one-half of the 1943 Detroit race rioters to the upper junior and senior high school age ranges, probably including many of 16 years and more, beyond the compulsory attendance age. Children are quite unlikely to take part

in disorders in school, but when they are released they contribute recruits to the rioting gangs.

4. Through leading civic, religious, trade union, and other organizations, *bring sufficient pressure to assure the dissemination of accurate reports and constructive official statements* over the radio stations, in the schools and churches, at civic and union meetings, and in the newspapers.

5. Above all, *if you are in a position of authority, do not experiment with half-way measures.* A race riot in a city is dynamite! Recognize the inadequacies of your government with a frankness that would be impolitic in ordinary times. Realize that in such a situation the public— your constituency—will expect, demand, and (oddly enough) reward decisive action. And do all in your power to dramatize the fact that equal justice *is being done* to the rioters and "innocent bystanders" of *both* races.

4. HOW TO CHANGE BASIC ANTI-NEGRO AND ANTI-WHITE PATTERNS

This book describes in detail the grave race riots during one week in one city. It brings to bear conclusions based upon riots in Los Angeles, Harlem, and elsewhere. And it then attempts to outline a program of prediction and prevention for *race riots generally.* No pretense is made that a program restricting itself to race riots is an adequate approach to the solution of the problems of Negro-white relations. It is directed merely at the worst inter-racial frictions and does not attempt to cope with basic conditions. In other words, this book is directed toward emergency measures to meet emergency crises, not toward long-term modifications of human relations.

Without pretending to go into the tremendous complications of a long-term policy, it will be helpful to relate emergency tactics to broader program perspectives.

As has been suggested, the elimination of the worst inter-racial frictions will permit healthy patterns of Negro-white relations to develop, but it is not enough to permit "nature to take its course." As Professor E. B. Reuter points out in his *American Race Problem:* the Negro is in constant danger of losing ground gained, especially during "back to normalcy" drives of the Harding type after wars and during financial depressions. Positive programs making for greater equalization of educational opportunities, of medical facilities, of housing and recreation, and of police and sanitation require constant energizing to keep them from succumbing to the gigantic pressures exerted against relieving Negroes of some of their special racial handicaps which our society has given to them.

This is really calling for a long-term program to combat the "fascist attitude of mind" to which Wendell L. Willkie attributed the Detroit race riots of 1943; and he called this attitude "the desire to deprive some of our citizens of their rights—economic, civic or political," and said that it "causes men to seek to rule others by economic, military or political force through prejudice."

We need to invest our energies more wisely by thinking in terms of thousands upon thousands of ways to promote decent inter-racial relationships. Women who have employed "white-women Negroes" for years as maids and laundresses delude themselves into thinking that they know something about the Negro people. They would be shocked and dismayed to learn how mistaken their impressions have been. They, most other white people, and a lot of Negroes would do well to find ways in which to learn something accurate and sympathetic about the kind of folks both races include.

We can advocate and eventually achieve the elimination of anti-Negro discrimination in the enlistment of police, firemen, and other governmental employees so that our governments will not appear to Negroes to be so overwhelmingly white-controlled. We can take immediate measure to help Negroes to get more adequate housing, and at a figure comparable to what their white neighbors must pay. We can prevail upon those labor unions which discriminate against Negro applicants to end this Nazi-like guarantee of white privilege.

White Americans might well ask themselves: Why do whites *need* so many special advantages in their competition with Negroes? Similar tactics for the elimination of Jewish competition in Nazi Germany brought the shocked condemnation of the civilized world. The mere fact that the abuses of the Negro are of so much longer standing does not alter the character of the relationship. Let us recognize, with Mr. Willkie, that our treatment of the Negro "has the same basic motivation as actuates the fascist mind when it seeks to dominate whole peoples and nations." It would be more to our credit to compete with Negroes on even terms.

These points suggest in general the character of desirable longterm perspectives. It is not necessary to catalogue detailed practices. After all, the program was laid out almost two milleniums ago by Jesus

Christ when He said that "all things whatsoever ye would that men should do to you, do ye even so to them."

The three most constructive lessons of the Detroit week of June 20, 1943, point to three effective ways of implementing the Golden Rule, three of the most practical objectives that emerge as goals for a long-term program. These objectives in the fields of (1) living, (2) learning, and (3) working point vividly to the virtue of the homely expression that "you can learn to like most anyone if you get to know him." Here are the senses in which we refer to living together, learning together, and working together:

1. Through experiences in neighborliness, or even in mere nearness, we can learn to live nearby people of another race without antagonistic racial frictions. In the Detroit riots, let us note again, observer after observer reported that no noteworthy trouble occurred in mixed districts where whites and Negroes had lived as neighbors long enough to get to know and understand each other.

2. Through the casual experience of classrooms and playgrounds, white and Negro children and adults can learn to associate with one another in schools and colleges without antagonistic racial frictions. Disorders between whites and blacks have taken place in Detroit's high schools, especially one that resulted in the stabbing of a student in 1941 at Northwestern High School. But that very uncommon incident emphasizes by its uncommonness the rule that schooltime associations diminish race frictions. After all, the students of Wayne University—in the heart of Detroit—went about their business on Monday, June 21, 1943, without any reported friction. "Going to school together" works powerfully against intolerance, especially when the school administrators and teachers count this lesson among their objectives.

3. Through the common experiences of shop work and union activity, whites and Negroes learn to appreciate each other's better qualities and to recognize their rights as fellow human beings. Here again occasional apparent exceptions develop, such as the Klan-inspired Packard strike that demanded the discriminatory treatment of Negroes, but the details of such cases indicate that they are not actual exceptions: the Packard strike was inspired by the Ku Klux Klan. As Major General Henry S. Aurand declared on Bloody Monday, there were no disturbances in the Detroit war plants, and U. S. Attorney General Francis Biddle later substantiated this observation.

These experiences offer hope of long-term Negro-white adjustments even though the faith of many in inter-racial peace is at a low ebb.

As one old Negro woman is quoted as saying, "There ain't no North any more. Everything now is South." But the industrialized and urbanized North has conditions of population-fluidity and of mixed living, learning, and working that will prevent the kinds of serfdom one finds in the agricultural areas of the South. With the increasing industrialization and urbanization of the South, it might more accurately be said, "Some day there won't be any North or South any more. It will all be just the United States. And it will give any man who deserves it a decent break—regardless of 'race, creed, or previous condition of servitude'!" Let us hope that we can make the prevention of race riots and of lynchings a first great step in that direction.

SUGGESTED READINGS
Books:

Carlson, John Roy, *Under Cover* (New York: E. P. Dutton, 1943)

Carpenter, Marie Elizabeth, *The Treatment of the Negro in American History School Textbooks* (Menasha, Wisc.: George Banta, 1941)

Clayton, C. H., and G. S. Mitchell, *The Black Worker and the New Unions* (Chapel Hill: University of North Carolina Press, 1939)

Davie, Maurice Rea, *The Negro in the United States* (New York: McGraw-Hill, forthcoming)

Davis, Allison, and John Dollard, *Children of Bondage* (Washington: American Council on Education, 1940)

Embree, Edwin R., *American Negroes: A Handbook* (New York: John Day, 1942)

Frazier, E. Franklin, *The Negro Family in the United States* (Chicago: University of Chicago Press, 1939)

Johnson, Charles S., *Patterns of Negro Segregation* (New York: Harper, 1943)

Lee, Alfred McClung, and Elizabeth Briant Lee, *The Fine Art of Propaganda* (New York: Harcourt, Brace, and the Institute for Propaganda Analysis, 1939)

McWilliams, Carey, *Brothers Under the Skin* (New York: Little Brown, 1943)

The Negro Caravan: Writings by American Negroes, selected and edited by Sterling A. Brown, Arthur P. Davis, and Ulysses Lee (New York: Dryden Press, 1941)

Ottley, Roi, *New World A-Coming: Inside Black America* (New York: Houghton, Mifflin, 1943)

Reuter, Edward B., *The American Race Problem* (New York: Thomas Y. Crowell, 1938)

Sterner, Richard, *The Negro's Share* (New York: Harper, 1942)

Willkie, Wendell, *One World* (New York: Simon & Schuster, 1943)

Pamphlets and Periodicals:

"The American Negro in World Wars I and II," Summer Edition of *The Journal of Negro Education,* Vol. XII, No. 3 (1943)

Blueprint for the American Community (New York: National Conference of Christians and Jews, n.d.)

Brown, Earl, and George R. Leighton, *The Negro and the War* (New York: Public Affairs Committee, 1942)

The C.I.O. and the Negro Worker (Washington: Congress of Industrial Organizations, n.d.)

"Color—Unfinished Business of Democracy," Special Race Edition of *Survey Graphic* (New York, November, 1942)

Eleazer, R. B., *Understanding Our Neighbors* (Atlanta: Conference on Education and Race Relations, 1942)

Federal Council of Churches, *To End This Strife* (New York: Federal Council of Churches, 1943)

Feldman, Herman, "The Techniques of Introducing Negroes Into the Plant," *Personnel* (New York: American Management Association, September, 1942)

Ford, James W., *The War of the Negro People* (New York: Workers Library Publishers, 1942)

Gilligan, Rev. Francis J., *Negro Workers in Free America* (New York: Paulist Press, 1939)

How Management Can Integrate Negroes in War Industries (New York State War Council, Committee on Discrimination in Employment, 1942)

"Minority Peoples in a Nation at War," edited by J. P. Shalloo and Donald Young, *The Annals of the American Academy of Political and Social Science,* Vol. CCXXIII (Philadelphia, September, 1942)

National Association for the Advancement of Colored People, *The Acid Test for Democracy* (New York: N.A.A.C.P., 1943)

National Negro Congress, *Defense Training Jobs and Negroes, Our War-Time Responsibility and Opportunity* (Washington: National Negro Congress, 1942)

The Negro and Defense (New York: Council for Democracy, 1941)

"The Negro Asks About Democracy," *Propaganda Analysis* (New York: The Institute for Propaganda Analysis, August, 1941)

The Negro Worker (New York: American Management Association, 1942)

Out of the Many—One (New York: Service Bureau for Intercultural Education, 1943)

U. S. Manpower Commission, *Manpower: One Tenth of a Nation* (Washington: U. S. Government Printing Office, 1942)

U. S. Office of War Information, *Negroes and the War* (Washington: Office of War Information, 1942)

White, Walter, "Behind the Harlem Riot," *New Republic* (New York, August 16, 1943, pp. 220-222)

White, Walter, and Thurgood Marshall, *What Caused the Detroit Riot?* (New York: N.A.A.C.P., 1943)